"This book is an important part of history that needs to be told. I was a German POW at Camp Pickett in November of 1944, and at Fort Indiantown Gap from December of 1944 to March 1946."

—Ernst Rinder, Lititz, Pennsylvania, proud
   to be a US citizen since 1961

"A sweet and lively story, *Captive* introduces young readers to the impact of war on civilians, and the little-known story of German POWs living and working in the US during WWII."

—John D. Roth, professor of history, Goshen College
   Editor, *The Mennonite Quarterly Review*
   Director, Mennonite Historical Library

"With his father off fighting the Nazis and his mother working away, John Witmer's teenage world is unsettled enough, when he suddenly finds himself spending his summer on a Mennonite farm among enemy prisoners of war. In this delightful story of unexpected friendships, an array of Americans and Germans, teens and parents, soldiers and pacifists all help each other find the courage to risk kindness, trust their gifts, and be themselves."

—Steven M. Nolt, Young Center for Anabaptist and
   Pietist Studies, Elizabethtown College

"Young adolescent readers will identify with John, who has a gift for drawing and is beginning to realize how this gift has the power to shape his sense of self and the relationships of those around him. At another level, readers of any age will find a dramatic account of a forgotten piece of history when more than 400,000 German prisoners of war were hosted in this country during World War II. This story sheds light on the complex perceptions about POWs in a southeastern Pennsylvania farming community."

—Rolando Santiago, Former Executive Director,
   Lancaster Mennonite Historical Society

CAPTIVE

Donna J. Stoltzfus

4880 Lower Valley Road · Atglen, PA 19310

Cover Design by Brenda McCallum

Type set in Eraser/Minion

ISBN: 978-0-7643-5551-6
Printed in the United States of America

Published by Schiffer Publishing, Ltd.
4880 Lower Valley Road
Atglen, PA 19310
Phone: (610) 593-1777; Fax: (610) 593-2002
E-mail: Info@schifferbooks.com
Web: www.schifferbooks.com

For our complete selection of fine books on this and related subjects, please visit our website at www.schifferbooks.com. You may also write for a free catalog.

Schiffer Publishing's titles are available at special discounts for bulk purchases for sales promotions or premiums. Special editions, including personalized covers, corporate imprints, and excerpts, can be created in large quantities for special needs. For more information, contact the publisher.

We are always looking for people to write books on new and related subjects. If you have an idea for a book, please contact us at proposals@schifferbooks.com.

Other Schiffer Books on Related Subjects:
Secret of Belle Meadow by Mary McVicker, ISBN: 978-0-87033-554-9
Oyster Moon by Margaret Meacham, ISBN: 978-0-87033-459-7

To Reuben and Dorothy Stoltzfus, my grandparents,
who lived their faith in everyday moments

And to Dave, Thomas, Helena, and Greta, who fill our home
to overflowing with books

When once again the tomatoes ripen
Eager hands will harvest them
They will again fill baskets and carts
Then we will remember this year

And as you harvest corn by the sweat of your brow
Again in the coming year
And as the stalks nod on acres and fields
They give you greetings from the old world

A little bit of home we have found here
And in the future our thoughts will be with you
May God keep you safe from danger
You are all very dear to us

Karl Demmler, Camp Reading, 1945

PREFACE

During World War II, hundreds of thousands of German and Italian prisoners of war were captured in Europe and North Africa. England asked the US to share the burden of providing accommodations for the men. POWs began arriving by ship in the US in late 1942. Eventually, there were more than 500 camps across the country, holding more than 400,000 POWs.

Throughout the book I refer to the prisoners of war as POWs or PWs. POW was the formal way to refer to a prisoner of war. Local farmers, however, would more often refer to the men as PWs.

As the US gained experience in running prisoner-of-war camps, it was discovered that pro-Nazi soldiers needed to be kept separate from nonpolitical and anti-Nazi soldiers. Violence, even murder, could take place when these men were housed in the same camps.

Ernst Rinder was a German POW in the US. He arrived by ship at Norfolk, Virginia, in 1944, and was sent to Camp Pickett in Blackstone, Virginia. As he walked down Main Street into Camp Pickett, he and the other newly arrived POWs were greeted by Afrika Korps soldiers. Afrika Korps soldiers were considered to be hardened Nazis. "They were dressed in German uniforms and were giving the Sieg Heil—the Nazi salute," Ernst said. "It seemed like there were hundreds of them. They looked like a long fence."

It didn't take long for the new arrivals to realize that their lives were in danger, as some of the Afrika Korps POWs accused them of being deserters. The men asked for protective custody and a transfer to a different camp. They were placed in separate quarters, outside the camp, until they could be sent to Fort Indiantown Gap in Pennsylvania. "The Fort Indiantown Gap camp was very different," said Ernst. "It was a more docile camp. There were no Nazi types there. Men were just happy to be alive and most were not looking for trouble."

With so many American men away at war, there was a severe labor shortage in the US. Even though there was initially fear that POWs would try to escape, the US government decided that the men were needed for jobs outside of the camps. They were sent to work on military bases, conservation projects, in factories, and on farms. They were paid for their labor. Most of the POWs did not attempt escape and enjoyed having the freedom to work.

In the summer of 1945, Daniel Glick, a tomato farmer in Smoketown, Pennsylvania, put in a request for POWs to help at his farm. The oldest Glick son, Isaac, drove to a camp at the Reading Army Air Field five days a week to get a "pick-up truck load" of German POWs. One of the POWs joked that "Isaac drives like a fire engine."

Vernon Glick, a younger son on the farm, said, "I was a young teenager during the summer of 1945, when German POWs worked on our farm during the tomato harvest. The actual fighting was overseas, but on the home front there were strong feelings about the morality of the war. Were conscientious objectors 'yellow bellies,' and should they be allowed some type of alternate service to our country? How should POWs be treated while in captivity? Some of the younger prisoners (Nazis) were still in fighting mode, and the guard assigned to our farm made very clear when they arrived in the morning what the work situation would be like for that day. Other POWs were trustworthy and glad to receive kindness (including some good food). They showed appreciation and worked hard in return."

Reuben G. Stoltzfus, my grandfather, was the manager of the cannery at the Glick farm during this time. He was raised Amish and knew enough Pennsylvania German to communicate with the POWs. My grandfather and the Glick family developed trusting relationships with some of the men. Karl Demmler, one of the POWs from East Germany, remembers this time fondly. "My stay in Lancaster County was the event of my life," said Demmler. "This friendship, without any prejudice, had been worth all the trouble. They never made me feel like a prisoner. It was one of the best times of my life."

Karl came back to the US four times to visit my grandparents and the Glick family. As a young girl, I met Karl and his wife on one of their trips. When I began to consider writing a novel about this time period, I contacted Karl, who shared stories with me about his experiences during the war. Some of those events inspired scenes in this book: The Americans gave Karl a cigarette when they captured him. Karl learned Old English calligraphy at a class he took at a prison camp in Colorado. He wrote names in the Glick family Bible. Before they returned to Europe after the war, the PWs gave the Glicks a book with artwork, notes, and poems as a thank you for how they were treated on the farm.

I wrote *Captive* to capture a glimpse of history that does not seem well-known among younger generations in the US. I also wrote it to honor personal stories that family and friends shared with me.

The novel is a fictional account. I relied on research and interviews to make the time period as historically accurate as possible. Any factual errors are my own.

ACKNOWLEDGMENTS

I began researching and writing this book many years ago, when my children were young and dialogue and plot ideas would come to me at odd moments. The story was written, gathered dust, edited, and reedited over a span of approximately twelve years. Thanks to all who read pages, answered my questions, and gave encouraging and wise input at various points in time: Duane Stoltzfus, Doris Stoltzfus, Helena Neufeld, Dave Neufeld, Ernie Neufeld, Thomas Neufeld, Katie Rodda, Karen Sherer Stoltzfus, Deb Roedema, Steve Coupland, Ruth Rinder, Stanley Carnarious, Brinton Rutherford, Julia Rutherford, Cal Esh, Ruth Martin, Phil Jantzi, Shannon Paris, Beky Weidner; my book club: Cheryl Weber, Rebecca Burkholder, Audrey Roth Kraybill, Beth Oberholtzer, Andrea Martin, Kristina Martin; my writing group: Ruth Ann Kulp, Wayne Martin, Jess Weiser, Angelina Horst; SCBWI Red-Eye group: Susan Denney, Mark Weaver, Laura Weller, Suzanne Mattaboni; Highlights Foundation Historical Fiction Workshop: Carolyn Yoder, Jeff Lantos, Claire Griffen, Liz Djupe, Martha Hewson, Joan Broerman, Gail Hoff, Marcia Melton, Janet Shultz; my editors at Schiffer Publishing: Tracee Groff, Cheryl Weber.

I would also like to thank those who shared their personal stories and helped me with research: Karl Demmler, Ernst Rinder, Dorothy Stoltzfus, Dale Stoltzfus, Vernon Glick, Isaac Glick, Millie Glick, Alyson Pursell Photography, Frank Peachey, MCC Records; The Lancaster Mennonite Historical Society. My apologies to anyone I've forgotten to mention.

PROLOGUE

June 1944
Camp Pickett, Virginia
Prisoner of War Camp

"Auch wir passen auf dich auf."

Hans opened his eyes. *We're watching you, too?* The angry whisper, a mouth with foul garlic breath, so close to his face, made him lay still but fully alert on his cot.

How had they sneaked up on him? He prided himself on sleeping like a soldier—quick to wake, always aware of danger—even danger that came from a fellow German soldier.

For a second he thought of reaching up and grabbing the neck that was within his reach, but he didn't know how many of them there were.

"You heard me," the man said now, the deep German voice no longer whispering. Hans listened to retreating footsteps and the door clicking shut. He continued to lay still. Why was he being targeted?

"We're watching you, too," the man had said. Why? Who else were they watching? Had something happened?

Now Hans sat up. He looked to his right. The bed was empty. Wilhelm was gone.

"You can't do anything," another bunkmate spoke up. "You try to help him, you'll be dead."

Hans quickly climbed out of the narrow bed and put on his shoes. "Then I'm dead," he said.

He pushed open the door and stood outside in the humid Virginia air. This prison camp was large. Where would they take him?

He heard scuffling noises. It sounded like they were coming from around the corner of the bunkhouse. He inched along, keeping his back to the wall.

Drops of sweat snaked along the crevices of his face. How many would he have to fight? Would his life end here? How ironic to survive a hideous war, only to be murdered by his own Nazi countrymen.

He pushed closer to the wall as he saw three figures hurry across the yard.

A moan, low and long, pinpointed a location. He ran around to the side of the building and saw Wilhelm lying on the ground.

Hans dropped to his knees. "It's me. Hans," he said in a hushed voice. "Try to be quiet. You don't want them coming back." Hans looked Wilhelm over. "Your nose looks broken. We have to stop the bleeding. Where else are you hurt?"

"Hard to breathe . . . kicked . . . my ribs." Wilhelm gasped. "A warning, they said . . . for not being loyal, for being a traitor. I was reading a book on American law . . . speaking English with the guards."

"You want to report it? Get medical help?"

"Dieter Klein was one of them," Wilhelm said. Hans leaned in closer to hear. "Get worse . . . if I report . . . just get me back to my bunk."

CHAPTER ONE

John couldn't believe his ears. He didn't mind working, but living away from home? "You'll be going to Elam Miller's farm for the rest of the summer," his mother had just told him. "You go to school with his daughter, Sarah. Your brother's going to the Souder farm. There aren't enough men to work with so many gone to war, and the farmers need your help. They'll come for you around six tomorrow morning."

John wanted to remind his mother that he was a thirteen-year-old boy. If he were a man he'd gladly be off fighting the Nazis like Pop was, not going to work on some Mennonite farm in Pennsylvania only a few miles from his home. But he guessed his mother didn't need to hear him pining to go to war. His older brother, Ben, was planning to join the army in six months, and his mother couldn't even talk about it.

Instead he packed a few items in a bag, including a tin of pencils. He placed his sketchbook next to the bag. His teacher had given him a new sketchbook for doing chores around the schoolhouse. She must have seen him drawing on scraps of paper since he had filled up all the pages in his other book. It was the best gift she could have given him.

John paused to listen to the ticking of the grandfather clock in the hallway. John, Ben, and his dad had finished building the clock the week before his dad left for Germany. That was more than a year ago. Now the paint was chipping on the "Closed" sign on the door of Ted Witmer's Furniture Shop, the family business behind their house. John was planning to fix it before his dad came home, whenever that was.

It had seemed like the ticking clock grew louder the day his dad left. Sometimes it was comforting to be reminded of him in that constant way, but other times John couldn't stand the sound. The tick-tick-tick reminded him that time was passing, Pop was gone, and he couldn't forget the war for even one second.

John walked toward the clock and ran his hand down its smooth cherry wood. He pressed his nose into an indented curve. The clock still held the faint scent of fresh-cut wood. Pop's clothes used to smell that way.

That night John broke the rules and let Pepper, his black lab, jump up on his bed. John slept with the warm dog curved into his stomach, one arm wrapped around Pepper's body.

When Jake Miller, Sarah's brother, pulled into the driveway in the morning, his mother followed John outside and gave him a long, smothering hug. He squirmed away and climbed into the pick-up truck. He knew his cheeks and neck would have a patchy, reddish flush, like they always did when he was embarrassed. He didn't look at Jake.

"Let me know when we get a letter from Pop!" he called out the window as stones began to crunch under the moving tires.

Even with the windows down, the inside of the truck smelled like ripe tomatoes, the kind split open and almost spoiled. An excited voice blared from the radio.

"Hitler was bruised and burned, but managed to escape a bombing plot to assassinate him," the radio announcer exclaimed. "We're hearing some type of explosives were used, maybe dynamite. Several of Hitler's military leaders were badly injured. Seems like they just missed their mark!"

"I wonder if that would have ended the war," Jake said. "Or if it would have kept going without him."

John couldn't believe they'd almost had him. If they'd known where he was going to be, if they were close enough to plant a bomb, why not just shoot him?

Jake turned onto a long dirt lane. Green cornstalks grew in neat rows to the right of the lane. To the left John saw six glass greenhouses and an off-kilter building with a tin roof built along the side of a hill. He knew they canned tomatoes and meat there. He had been to the farm once before, on a school outing to see the canning operation.

Jake parked in front of a two-story, white clapboard house. Sarah, the oldest Miller daughter, stood leaning on the porch railing. Sarah was the same age as John, though John would turn fourteen in a couple of weeks. They had been in the same class for years, but John wouldn't really call her a friend. He didn't think they had a thing in common.

"Hi John," she said, her green eyes squinting slightly in the sun. "I'll set your bag inside for you. You can have a seat on the porch if you want. We need to catch chickens before breakfast, but we have to wait for my dad to bring a crate."

John handed Sarah his bag but held on to his sketchbook. He might as well draw while he was waiting. The Miller farm was like the kind featured on postcards, making you feel that the world was right with itself, an orderly and peaceful place.

Sarah put his bag inside, then walked back onto the porch. Every day she wore her blond hair in a bun, but it always seemed a little out of control. The wind blew a loose strand across her cheek. John wanted to capture that motion she had, when she would catch a wayward curl and impatiently try to tuck it back into the bun with a bobby pin.

John made quick strokes with his pencil. If he'd owned watercolors, he would have loved to work color and light into Sarah's green eyes as she stood watching him, fidgeting with her hair.

"If you're drawing me, I'd like very much to see it when you're done," she said. "In school, you're always drawing and hardly let anyone see your work."

John looked at Sarah's face taking shape on the page. Something wasn't quite right.

"What do you do with all your drawings, anyway?" Sarah asked.

"Could you move back to where you were?" John asked, as Sarah bent down to pet a barking beagle that had run onto the porch.

Sarah sighed but stood up and leaned against the railing once more. "I won't be doing this all summer, you know," she said. "Anyway, you'll probably soon have other interesting people to draw."

"Like who?" John asked.

"War prisoners."

John stopped drawing. "What do you mean?"

"We're getting some German soldiers from a prisoner of war camp. They're going to help pick tomatoes. We need the extra hands."

John stared at her, his blue eyes intense and unblinking.

"What's the matter with you?" Sarah asked, as she swatted a fly away from her face. "Haven't you heard about the POWs getting out to work?"

"I can't believe your father would bring those men here. How could you stand to be around them?"

"*Ach*, John, they'll just be working here. They can sit at a prison and do nothing, or they can help us work. My dad isn't the first farmer to ask for war prisoners."

"I know that. But it's one thing to read about it in the newspaper and another thing to actually be around them."

"I'd rather have those men around than lose half our harvest because we don't have enough help."

"They'll send armed guards, you know. Think you'll like that? Men walking around your farm with guns?"

"No, I won't like that," Sarah said. "But we'll put up with it."

John felt like shaking Sarah, with her simple answers. It didn't matter to her that these men were the enemy. The men coming here might have fought against his dad, might have tried to kill his dad. Who knows how many lives they had ruined in their march to take over Europe? How could he casually pick tomatoes next to them?

"I won't stay here if they come," John said.

Sarah pinched her lips together. "You surprise me, John."

"I surprise you? Because I don't want to work with Nazis?"

"It's time to get going, my dad just put a crate outside of the chicken shed," Sarah said as she began to walk past John.

John stood up and grabbed her arm. "When are they coming?"

"I don't know for sure. Tomorrow maybe."

"I won't be here. I'd rather go hungry."

"Then you'd better eat a good breakfast," Sarah said, pushing his hand off her arm. "Since you're soon going to be starving yourself."

John kicked a stone from the porch before he began to follow Sarah. He couldn't believe German POWs were coming here. It'd be one thing if they would be treated the way they deserved to be treated. But he knew Elam and Anna Miller wouldn't act mean to anyone. And he could just see Sarah mixing with them, like they were interesting new neighbors she wanted to learn to know.

John's stomach growled. He'd only eaten a couple of crackers before Jake picked him up. There wasn't much to eat at his house, but he sure didn't need Sarah finding that out.

In Pop's last letter, he had talked about being hungry all the time. About what he'd give for one of mom's home cooked meals. That was saying something, because John didn't think his mom was a very good cook. But that letter came weeks ago.

John decided to put in a day's work and then leave. He'd walk home if he had to. Maybe a new letter would come from Pop today. His mom would be so happy, she wouldn't care when John told her he wasn't going back to the Millers.

CHAPTER TWO

"Just go on in," Sarah said, motioning to a wooden shed. "There's the crate. We need a dozen chickens. I'll help you as soon as I'm done feeding the dogs."

John walked into the chicken coop. He resisted the impulse to pinch his nose closed. Standing still, he tried to adjust to the sharp odor of chicken manure trapped within four walls of dense, unmoving heat. He could almost feel the smell seeping into his skin, and figured he'd carry the stench with him for the rest of the day.

The chickens gathered at the far end of the shed. John slowly approached a bird. He'd never caught chickens before in his life. Should he grab it by the legs? By the neck? He looked into the black, panicked eyes of the bird he was trying to corner.

"I know how you feel, buddy," he said.

He heard a latch click and knew Sarah was behind him, watching.

"Are you afraid of them?" she asked. John heard the amazement in her voice.

"I've never done this before."

"Just grab them," Sarah said, entering the pen. "Like this."

Sarah walked slowly toward a group of chickens. They grew uneasy, fluttering their wings and scurrying around the straw-covered floor as she cornered one and quickly grabbed its legs. It squawked loudly as it was flipped upside down, joining the other chickens in a rising chorus of panic. John sneezed as kicked-up straw dust settled into his nostrils. One chicken flew up under Sarah's long dress. With her free hand she flipped her hem to get it out.

"There," she said, as she shoved the captured chicken into the crate.

The chicken complained, letting loose high-pitched screeches and thumping around in the cage. John felt sorry for it, but would never admit that. He knew he would hate this job, even if he got good at it.

John lunged for a chicken and cringed as he wrapped his hand around a skinny leg. "Ow!" he said. "That beak is sharp!"

"Of course it is," Sarah replied. "So don't let 'em peck you."

Gritting his teeth, John pushed the bird into the crate, trying to keep the others from escaping. The chicken seemed more like a woodpecker, the way it went after his arm.

"There are worse jobs, John," Sarah said. "At least you're not off fighting. I bet your dad would rather be catching chickens."

"I don't think so," John said. This girl thought she knew so much. "My dad's a soldier. He believes in what he's doing."

Sarah didn't respond. John knew Sarah's family didn't believe in fighting. Her older brother Sam was doing some kind of service work in a hospital in Philadelphia instead of fighting in the war. John wondered if Jake was going to take off for Philadelphia too when it was his turn to go to war.

"Someone's got to stop the Nazis," John said. "What if Hitler invaded America? Then you'd be glad for the men who'd pick up guns to defend you."

"Maybe," Sarah said. "But it still doesn't make me think killing is right. There," she said, as she shoved the twelfth chicken into the crowded crate and latched the cage door.

"Fun job," John said.

"At least now you know how to do it."

"I know how to get pecked, that's for sure."

"I can always teach the POWs how to catch them," Sarah said. "They won't be scared of them, I bet."

CHAPTER THREE

John waited for Sarah to finish washing her hands at the outdoor sink. He stank like chickens, but at least he could scrub his hands clean. The yellowish bar of soap looked homemade. It felt rough on his hands, but he rubbed it hard over his skin.

"You trying to take a layer off?" asked Sarah, standing with her hands on her hips.

"I like clean hands before I eat," answered John. Had Sarah always been this irritating or was he just on edge? John wasn't sure, but almost everything she said was working on his nerves.

Mrs. Miller stood at the stove in the kitchen, flipping eggs. She peered over her shoulder at the sound of the screen door banging shut.

"Hello, John!" Mrs. Miller gave him a wide smile. "My, you've grown! You must be over six feet—a few inches taller than Sarah now."

"Hi, Mrs. Miller." John smiled back. John knew Mrs. Miller from school picnics over the years. Mrs. Miller looked so different from Sarah. She was short and her face reminded him of a bowl of rising dough, full and round and soft-looking, with asymmetrical dimples to make it interesting. Her warm, brown eyes always seemed to hone in on a person with anticipation, making you want to share things with her.

"How is your mother, John? Was this morning hard for her, with you leaving to come here?" she asked.

"I don't know, Mrs. Miller. She seemed okay. She's going to try to get a job in town, at the factory."

"Well, more and more women are working in the factories, that's for sure."

Mrs. Miller set a platter of eggs and bacon on the table. Sarah added a pitcher of milk. She didn't look at John as she sat down across from him. What was she so miffed about? That he said he was leaving? John felt like he was the one who had a right to be mad.

"Dorothy! Kenny!" Mrs. Miller called toward the stairs. "Come right now!"

A younger version of Sarah came running into the kitchen, her brother right behind her. They both tried to sit in the chair next to John. Dorothy caught the edge of the chair, almost tipping into John's lap.

"What in the world?" Mrs. Miller stood with her hands on her hips. "Kenny Miller, go sit quietly next to Sarah. You can sit next to John at supper tonight. My lands. You'd think we never get company."

Dorothy grinned at John. She was missing two front teeth. John had to grin back.

When Mr. Miller bustled into the kitchen and sat down, the group grew quiet.

"Bless this house, Lord, and all those seated around this table. We pray for John's family, that they remain safe and well. Thank you for bringing John to us and for all the help he'll be. Bless this food. Amen."

John opened his eyes to Sarah's pointed gaze. He stared back at her a few seconds, and then raised his glass of water to his mouth. She wouldn't change his mind about leaving with that look.

"John, would you mind helping Sarah watch the children this morning?" asked Mrs. Miller. "We have some women coming to help pick tomatoes who have younger children. Not babies, but young enough to need watching."

"Sarah likes to read to them. Give them a little schooling," added Mr. Miller. "Isn't that right, Sarah?"

Sarah nodded at her plate.

John tried not to look disappointed. He didn't mind kids, but he was hoping to work at the cannery the Millers ran. They cooked tomatoes and put them in large cans. They sold the cans to the Campbell Soup Company. The Millers also canned meat to sell. He knew there were pulleys and interesting gadgets and equipment in the cannery. He thought it might be fun to work in there.

"Come on, John!" Dorothy grabbed his hand as soon as she was excused from the table, and started toward the door. "Sarah has to do the dishes first."

"Thanks for breakfast, Mrs. Miller," John said, resisting Dorothy's pulling hand. "It was really good." John hadn't felt this full for a long time. At home, when the food ran out, his mother would smile and say, "We had just enough. I planned that just right." John never told her when he was still hungry. There wasn't any food left anyway.

"Just a minute, Dorothy, I want to get something." John ran upstairs to grab some extra scrap paper and his tin of pencils. Maybe the kids would like to draw.

He took the two children outside and walked with them to a grassy spot on the side of the house.

"Sit still, Dorothy, and I'll draw a picture of you."

"Can we draw too?" Kenny asked, as he tried to pick up an ant.

"Sure, there's paper over here."

John's favorite thing to draw was people. He liked it best when his subjects didn't even know he was drawing. He could sketch quickly, capturing facial expressions with fine, intricate strokes. It had driven his brother Ben crazy sometimes. John would sketch him chewing a pencil, reading, working, talking. He even drew him once when he was in the outhouse and had left the door open a crack. Ben tore that one up.

"Maybe you should get to work instead of following me around," Ben would say. "I'm not doing your chores." But John always got his work done. He just finished later than Ben, taking time to draw in between. His dad would get more impatient than Ben, even raising his voice sometimes. But his mom would smooth things over if she was around. She'd look over John's shoulder while he was working and say, "Don't throw that out, now. That's a nice one."

"Let me see, let me see!" Dorothy said, hopping up after a few seconds.

"Sit down for one more minute, just like you were."

"But this takes too long."

Kenny came up behind John to watch. "Hey! That looks like you, Dorothy! Come here and see!"

"No!" John knew they were just little kids, but he was getting frustrated. "I'm not finished."

But Dorothy was already up and looking at the sketch of her face.

"I like it." She plucked the drawing out of John's hand. "I want to show my dad."

"Not now, Dorothy," John said. "Give the drawing back to me."

But Dorothy had already begun to run toward the greenhouse where Mr. Miller had headed after breakfast. Kenny ran after her.

"Wait!" John yelled. He gathered the pencils and put them inside the case.

Sarah walked up beside him. "What are you doing? Were you drawing?"

"A little bit."

"Can I see what you did?"

"I don't have it." John began to head toward the closest greenhouse in the row of six. He peered through the thick glass wall. "I think Kenny and Dorothy went in here."

"They're not supposed to play in the greenhouses, just so you know."

"They were looking for your dad."

"Well, he's not in there."

"I can see that." John ran a hand through his short, light, brown hair. There was no breeze this morning, and his hair stood up in patches, damp with sweat. He turned and saw a man carrying a crate of tomatoes.

"Who's that?"

"That's Reuben, our cannery manager. He's been here a few months. I'll introduce you."

Reuben had a baseball cap on his head, and wore a thick rubber apron. He was whistling, but stopped as they approached.

"Reuben, this is John. He's going to be helping around here. Well, for a little while, anyway." Sarah raised her eyebrows at John.

"Glad to hear it. We can sure use the help." Reuben set the crate down and reached out to shake John's hand.

"Are your children here yet?" Sarah asked.

"No, Lydia stayed home with them this morning. She'll probably stay home the rest of the week, too, with everything that'll be going on."

John felt his face tighten. He guessed Reuben's wife was staying home because of the POWs coming. At least she knew better than to bring her kids around Nazis. John needed to figure out a way to tell Mr. Miller he didn't want to be around them either.

CHAPTER FOUR

July 1944
Fort Indiantown Gap, Pennsylvania
Prisoner of War Camp

Hans ran his hand down the front of his work shirt. "I haven't had a breakfast like that in over ten years. Eggs, bacon, fresh milk, fruit, thick toast with melted butter. My stomach doesn't know what to think. I've had some good meals at the other camps—and this is my fourth—but the food here has been surprising."

"I keep waiting for it to change," said Fritz. "Like they're teasing us. We've only been here two weeks and I think I've gained a few pounds."

"You needed to," said Hans, as they watched several trucks line up outside the gates.

"They didn't clear Wilhelm to work on the farm."

"I heard. It's probably best. He needs to be fully healed before he's digging potatoes, or whatever they'll have us do. Besides," Hans tilted his head to the left, "it looks like Klein is going out."

Fritz looked over and stared at the back of Klein's head. He lowered his voice. "Don't they see what he's like? I couldn't believe he was transferred here. I hope we don't end up working together on the same farm."

Hans shrugged. "I don't know where he's assigned, but there's only one of him. At least from what I've seen. None of his Nazi comrades came along from Camp Pickett."

"This is the best camp I've been to," said Fritz. "I hope there's no trouble."

Hans pointed to a green pick-up truck. "I think that's our truck." They began to walk toward the young man who stood by its side holding a sign.

CHAPTER FIVE

"Early in the day and it's already hot," John complained, as he and Sarah stood on the porch after breakfast the next morning.

"You gonna walk home now?"

John could feel the intensity of Sarah's gaze, but he stared straight ahead. He had planned on going home yesterday after work, he really had, but when he had stepped into the kitchen at suppertime, Mrs. Miller was setting down a steaming bowl of mashed potatoes with brown butter melted on top.

"Sit here, John," Kenny had called to him. John knew he was being weak, but he sat down. And after eating two thick slices of meatloaf, how could he say he no longer wanted to stay there? John was disgusted with himself, but not disgusted enough to hold back from eating pancakes this morning.

Reuben approached the porch and nodded at John. "You wouldn't be looking for a job, would you? I could use a hand with some boxes."

John began to follow him when he heard a horn beep several times. He turned to watch dust billowing up around the Miller's rusted green pick-up truck as it wound its way up the dirt road toward the farm.

"Well, look at that," Reuben said slowly. "Looks like we've got plenty of hands now."

The truck came to a stop in front of the barn. Six men sat in a half circle in the truck bed, the brims of their caps facing forward. One man stood up and stretched, arms reaching upward, his back to John. In the middle of his dark-blue shirt were the letters "PW." John knew the PW stood for "prisoner of war." The large letters looked like they could have been painted on with stencils. When the other men began standing, John saw the white letters on their loose-fitting work pants and their sleeves. There was no mistaking who they were.

John took a few steps forward. He couldn't help himself. He felt as though a magnet was pulling him, making him face an enemy who was no longer abstract but young-looking men jumping off the back of a truck. John thought some of the PWs looked only a couple of years older than he was.

He felt Sarah walk up beside him. "What are you doing?" she asked quietly.

"Just looking."

The men began walking in single file, following Mr. Miller. An armed guard trailed behind. One by one the men passed John and Sarah. John shoved his trembling hands in his pockets. A short, stocky blond-haired PW glanced at them briefly, but John saw his eyes take in Sarah.

Each man noticed Sarah as they passed. John felt Sarah's dress brush against his arm as she inched closer to him. John looked at her. He'd never seen Sarah spooked by anything. And if she hadn't moved so close to him, he wouldn't know she was bothered by the men. She stood stiffly, with her chin up, and stared right back at them.

John guessed Sarah was used to men looking at her even though she was only thirteen. Sarah was the prettiest girl at school. She was tall—around five feet, eleven inches, a couple inches shorter than John, who was six feet, one inch—and thin and graceful looking, reminding John of an alert deer, the way she held her head sometimes. She seemed older than her age, and John thought the golden flecks in her grass-green eyes were her best feature, though he never planned on telling her that.

The last PW, a broad-shouldered man, taller than John, with dark hair that looked like it had been shaved not too long ago, stared the hardest as he slowed his steps. He looked older than the other PWs, and his narrowed eyes were sharply focused on Sarah. His gaze moved from her head to her toes and back up again.

John glared at the man. He felt his face begin to flush. This man was lucky to be out of the prison camp. Who did he think he was?

As if the PW had read his thoughts, he turned his head slightly to make eye contact with John before moving on.

John clenched his fist in his pocket, knowing he was powerless to use it.

"I read something in the newspaper about the PWs when they get out to work," Sarah whispered. "About how they stare at women and children. They don't see them very often. Some have gone a couple of years without seeing a woman or child. They just have to get used to me."

John shook his head. Sarah still acted as if having the men on the farm was of no concern to her. "Stay away from them, Sarah," he said sharply. "Especially the last one with the short, dark hair."

CHAPTER SIX

There was no way John was going to leave now. Sarah was so naïve. How could she be so book smart at school and so idiotic about the PWs?

He felt like he needed to stay to keep an eye on things. To look out for Sarah and the kids, since he couldn't trust her to do it herself. He could be like another guard. He wouldn't have a rifle, but at least he had his eyes.

"Excuse me, John."

John turned to see Reuben standing behind him. "I was hoping I'd get one or two of the PWs to help me out, but looks like they all have to stay together so the guard can keep watch. Would you be able to help me carry some boxes of meat to the freezer? We just had a delivery and the meat is sitting in that truck over there. I need to get it out of the sun and into the freezer."

"Go ahead, John," Sarah said. "We don't have many children today. I'll see to them."

"I have my stoves started," Reuben said, as John hurried after him. "I can't leave them unattended for long." Reuben pointed to a wooden shed. "The freezers are in there. You'll have to unload the meat from the boxes so it'll fit."

John relished the cold air that hit his face as he pushed pounds of pork wrapped in heavy white paper into the freezer. He squinted as he stepped back out into the bright sun, looking down as he walked back toward the boxes.

His eyes took in a pair of work shoes before he looked up into the face of the short, blond PW, holding a box of meat.

"You have a helper after all," Reuben called to him. "The guard said he's all right to work with us."

"*Wie heißt du?*" Reuben asked the PW. John recognized the Pennsylvania German sentence for "What's your name?" Sarah had said Reuben used to be Amish and hoped the PWs would be able to understand the low German he grew up speaking.

"Hans," the PW replied in a deep voice.

Reuben said something else to the PW, who smiled slightly and nodded. John felt like he was the outsider, not understanding what was being said.

Reuben turned to John. "You two share the same name, did you catch that? Hans is John in German."

"I didn't know that," said John. He didn't like it, either.

"Give a holler when you're done, John," Reuben said, before turning back to the cannery.

John stared at Hans for a few seconds. The light blue eyes that met his weren't mean-looking. Just steady. Steady and waiting for John to do something. Hans shifted the box to his shoulder.

John turned and walked back to the shed. He held the screen door open and motioned for Hans to follow him. He pointed to the floor near the freezer and Hans set the box down. This was strange, John thought, to be bossing around a German soldier. John pushed up the heavy freezer door and began to unload the meat. Hans stood behind him. John had goose bumps, and figured they were not just from the freezer. What if this man shoved him from behind? John knew he would just about fit in that large freezer. How did the guard know this man was all right?

John looked over his shoulder. He pointed to the freezer. The PW nodded and began stocking the meat. John pushed past him to go outside. Hans looked strong. He had wide shoulders and held the box of meat like it was easy. He must hate Americans and being a prisoner. What if he tried to escape? John didn't think of himself as a weakling, but he knew he wouldn't be a match for this soldier.

John pulled another box off of the truck. The box was wide, bulky, and heavy, but smaller than the one the PW had carried. John headed toward the shed as the PW pushed open the screen door. The distance to the shed wasn't more than twenty yards, but John thought the muscles in his arms would surely tear if he didn't soon put the meat down. He gritted his teeth, determined to make it past the PW, who stood by the door, holding it open.

But each step was getting slower, and Hans began to walk toward John. Their eyes met for a split second before Hans put his arms under John's box and lifted. John's face burned as he walked to open the shed door.

They worked in polite silence. They held the door open for each other, but John stayed outside when the PW was inside the shed. Hans seemed to understand this, and didn't enter the shed when John was inside.

As John approached the shed with the last box, he heard Hans's voice through the screen door.

"Why are you crying?" he asked in a thick German accent.

Hans spoke English?

John hesitated before entering the shed. Who was he talking to? John nudged the door open with his foot. Hans was in a crouching position, looking behind some empty, stacked crates in a corner.

John heard Dorothy's muffled voice. "I saw a scary man with a big gun walking behind my dad. Is my dad in trouble? Did the war come here?"

"No," answered Hans. "The war is far away. Over the ocean. Some men, like myself, came here to work. The man with the gun is a guard. But he's not guarding your father, just us workers."

"Dorothy!" John said, walking toward her. "Does anyone know you're in here?"

"No," she said, as she crawled around the crates. "'Cause I was playing hide-n-seek with Kenny. And when I got scared, I came to my best hiding place."

"You can't run off and hide like that without telling anyone," John said.

"We always play hide-n-seek," she said.

"You can't do that anymore. Not without Sarah or me knowing and playing, too. Okay?"

John glanced at Hans, guessing he understood every word. His knowing English changed things. Working in silence, with a language barrier, kept them separate. But now John had to choose whether or not to talk to him.

"Well, I'm done hiding anyway. I want to show . . . what's your name?" Dorothy asked Hans.

"Hans."

"I want to show Hans my picture."

"He's not interested, Dorothy."

Dorothy dug the drawing out of her pocket. "Look." She held out the paper to Hans. "John drew this. It's of me."

Hans studied the sketch for several seconds.

"It's not finished," John said, and looked away, rolling his eyes. What a stupid thing to say. Why should he care what the PW thought of his sketch? John ran his fingers through his hair. He wanted to snatch the drawing back. It was too personal—a drawing of Dorothy, his work, in the hands of this German.

"I could tell this was you, even if you hadn't told me," Hans handed the drawing back to Dorothy. "It's good." He looked at John as he said this. "Very good."

He spoke like he was some authority on art, John thought. He probably didn't know anything about it. Why give him these compliments? Why was he acting so nice?

"How old are you, Dorothy?" Hans asked.

"Five."

"A fine age," Hans said with a smile.

"C'mon, Dorothy," John grabbed her hand. "Let's go.

CHAPTER SEVEN

June 7, 1944
US Naval ship
France

"Ted, what's the name of your boy who likes to draw?" the man behind the easel asked. He took a step back on the deck of the ship, looking at his painting of the off-duty soldiers, who were playing cards several yards away.

Ted Witmer glanced at the artist before continuing to clean his rifle. "John. Why?"

"I'm almost finished here," the artist answered, dipping his brush in the bluish-green paint that matched the water lapping softly around them. "If you're interested, I'll draw you nice and quick. You could send it home to your family. Your boy might like it."

"Huh," Ted grunted, laughter edging into the sound. "John surely would like that. He'd be shocked I stood still for a drawing. I never did that for him at home."

"Why not? Was he that bad?"

"He can draw. That's never been the problem. All right, Al. I guess I'll do this. Where should I stand?"

"Right there's good. Put your helmet on, and look this way," Al instructed.

Ted held his rifle by his side. "I want to go play cards. Let's make this quick."

"Yeah, yeah." Al grinned. "So you've got a son with an artistic eye. That's one of the good Lord's best gifts, you know."

Ted stared straight ahead, over Al's shoulder. "The light won't last much longer," he said.

Al's hand was moving quickly, his eyes shifting up and down, from the man to the page. "You can tell a lot by drawing a man."

"Yeah? What can you tell?"

"Wait and see."

Ted watched the water wash over the sand on shore and withdraw back into itself. He would have liked this place in peaceful times, without feeling like death was just biding its time, tap dancing up and down his spine.

"Why do I get the feeling you don't like your boy being an artist?"

Ted pulled his thoughts back to John and felt an immediate tension. He didn't feel like telling Al he had never considered drawing a good way for a young boy to spend his time. A girl, maybe. But his son?

Other than that, John was a good boy. He'd be quick to sign up for the war if given a chance. Ted wondered if John would choose to be a combat artist like Al, drawing and painting scenes during wartime, or if he'd rather fight. John would want both, but Ted didn't think that would be possible.

"It gets in the way," Ted said after a moment. "He's always behind. Behind in his chores. Behind in his homework. Walks behind everyone. Stares off at things when you're talking to him. About drives me crazy. If you didn't know better, you'd think he's slow."

"Is he?"

"Not if you listen to his teachers. They say he's doctor smart. He could be whatever he sets his mind to. But you can't get that boy to focus on anything but drawing.

"Even his dog suffers. One time John's sitting at the table and his dog comes up and sits in front of him. John starts mumbling nonsense like, 'Hey Pepper, stay right there. I think you like being in my drawings. Hold on, I want to get that look in your eye.'

"That dog ain't looking at you with that pitiful expression because he wants you to draw him," I said. "He's sitting there 'cause you probably forgot to feed him again."

"'Sorry, Pepper,' he says."

Ted shook his head. "Can't tell you how many times we had that conversation, or one like it. He just has an absentminded head."

"What would I think if I saw his work?"

Ted's mouth curved, pride pulling up its edges. He reached into his pocket. "Here. He drew this of my wife."

Al walked over and took the piece of paper. He stared at the drawing of a woman—her wavy hair, the take-on-the-world tilt of her head with one hand on her hip, the hooded tiredness in her eyes, the soft texture of her dress.

"I'd like to meet your son." Al handed the drawing back to Ted. "He's better than I was at his age. But don't quote me on that. I never admit anyone is or was better than me." Al laughed. "He must be a stubborn son-of-a-gun, pursuing his artistic side with you around."

"Good. You meet my son and help him figure out how to make a living doodling on paper. No offense to you. You seem to be doing okay. But I don't know how that boy's going to eat or take care of a family. He'll be sitting and drawing his kids like he does Pepper. I don't want to see pictures of my grandchildren with hungry eyes."

"Seems like a lot of worrying."

"You done yet? I'm going to head over to that card game."

Al handed Ted the rough paper.

Ted stared for a moment at the drawing of himself staring off into the distance, eyes serious and steady. "My family will be happy to get it. Thank you."

Al began to put away his paints. "Help me carry this stuff to my bunk, would you?"

"That's the other end of the ship." Ted held on to his rifle and grabbed the folded-up easel with his free hand. He followed Al along the deck for almost an eighth of a mile. "Game'll be over by the time I get there."

Ted hesitated as they neared the ship's stairs. "Hear that?"

A droning sound had both men quickly looking up.

"Whose plane?" Al asked.

"Not ours."

The explosion rang out as they dove to the deck. They turned around to watch the bow of the ship splinter apart and then burst into flames, knowing their friends and the card game were smack in the middle of that ferocious, red heat.

CHAPTER EIGHT

John told Reuben they were done unloading the meat. He watched Hans walk into the greenhouse where the other PWs were working.

John took Dorothy's hand. "If we can't find Sarah, we can draw down by the stream, since you didn't get a chance to earlier."

"Who was that man I showed my picture to? He talked funny."

"He's from Germany, a country far away. He pronounces words different than you do because he speaks another language."

"Why does he have letters on his shirt?"

"So people know he's a German soldier. He was fighting against the Americans and was caught. They brought him here."

"So he's a bad man?"

"I don't know what kind of man he is," John said. "But I think he's done bad things." How could he explain this to a five-year-old? He didn't even want to try. "Just be careful around him," he said.

"Okay," Dorothy said. "But the man with the gun was scarier than him."

John sat with his back against a tree, his sketchbook on his lap. Dorothy's pencil moved slowly, as she tried to draw the shallow water moving seamlessly around the rocks in the stream in front of them.

The PWs came out of the greenhouse, carrying baskets of tomatoes toward the cannery. John noticed the one with the black hair didn't follow them but walked casually to the edge of the cornfield, and stood there, looking out.

Kenny ran up to John. "Sarah said I could come over," he said. "Can I have a paper?"

"Sure," John said, not taking his eyes off the PW. "Behind me is paper and a pencil. Draw something you see, like a tree or the stream."

John glanced at Kenny a few moments later and watched him draw a line down the center of his paper.

"What's the prison look like where the PWs stay?" Kenny asked.

"I don't know," said John. "What's that got to do with drawing trees?"

"Well, do they sleep on a floor or a bed? Do they ever change their clothes? Do they wear pajamas at night or sleep in the prisoner clothes they have on?"

"How would I know that?" John asked. "I've never been to the prison. And I'm not going to yell over there to that PW to ask him."

"Can I?" asked Kenny.

"Just draw something you can see."

"I am, mostly," said Kenny. "Half of my picture is going to be of the farm. But on the other side I want to draw the prison."

"Why?" asked John.

"I don't know," said Kenny. "I was just thinking about those men being here and then going back to a prison. Now I have to add a soldier. That one over there."

Kenny stood up and began walking closer to the PW.

"Kenny, get back here," John said. He couldn't figure out what that PW was doing, and why the guard didn't notice he was missing.

Kenny stopped walking and sat down. John sat beside him. The PW turned, giving them a side view of his face. John drew the taut way the man held his shoulders and head. He remembered the anger in the dark-colored eyes that had ogled Sarah, the thickness and slant of his eyebrows, the high cheekbones, which, John had to admit, helped define a handsome face. He tried to capture the edgy aloneness of this German soldier on Pennsylvania soil. On the back he wrote down the date. "July 21, 1944. Mid-morning. PW at edge of cornfield."

CHAPTER NINE

"Hey you! Klein!"

John turned to watch the guard walk over to the PW by the cornfield. He had his rifle tilted up. Not pointed at the man, but threatening.

"I need a translator!" the guard yelled over his shoulder. He pointed at Hans. "You speak English. Come over here!"

John inched closer as Hans walked slowly toward the guard.

"Ask him what he's doing here," the guard said.

Hans spoke to the other PW, Klein, who hadn't moved from his spot. He didn't look scared. He stood there like he had every right to.

"He said he's just looking," Hans said. "He said he's never seen a cornfield."

"Right," said the guard. "Tell him if he wanders off to stare at cornfields again, he won't be coming back tomorrow."

Klein stared at Hans with cold eyes as Hans relayed the guard's message.

"Let's go," said the guard, beckoning with his rifle.

A bell began to clang.

Sarah came around from the front of the house. "Time to eat!" she called, a smile on her face. "Kommt essen!" A slight breeze blew wisps of her hair back from her face, and her dress billowed gently against her legs.

John glanced at the men. Their eyes were on Sarah, as he knew they would be.

"Where are they eating?" he asked Sarah.

"The picnic tables around back of the house."

"You can follow me," John said to the guard, stepping forward in front of Sarah.

Sarah looked annoyed. "I'm capable of taking them to lunch," she said into John's ear, as she fell into step beside him.

"You shouldn't be around these men." Sarah wasn't even grateful he was trying to divert their attention away from her.

Sarah rolled her eyes. "You're so serious all the time, John."

"You can sit here," she called out to the men, pointing to the tables. "Max!"

John looked up to see Mrs. Miller running down the porch steps after their beagle, who was carrying something in his mouth.

"Help me, you two," she said to John and Sarah. "He has a pack of my good dried beef!"

John stepped forward, but he didn't feel like making a fool of himself by chasing a racing dog. John tried not to laugh as Mrs. Miller bustled around a picnic table. He had never seen Mrs. Miller run before. She moved pretty fast for being a heavyset woman. A PW John heard someone call Fritz was carrying his lunch to a table and tripped as Max darted in front of him. A small cloud of dry dirt rose up as he landed on his bottom.

"You better catch 'im, Anna, before he injures any of the men," Mr. Miller called out with a snort of laughter.

Like John, the PWs had been silently watching the dog's antics. But Mr. Miller's laughter set everyone off.

Mrs. Miller ignored them. "Now mind!" She pointed her finger at the dog. Max stood still, watching her, the package of meat in his mouth and his tail slowly wagging.

Fritz, who was still sitting on the ground, reached out and snatched the meat, wrapped in tattered paper, from Max's mouth.

"Thank you!" Mrs. Miller said. "No one else felt the call to help," she continued, looking at Mr. Miller and Sarah and shaking her head.

John was still grinning when he noticed Klein sitting by himself at the end of one of the tables. He was the only person not looking amused. He seemed to be studying the long lane, which led to the road. When he abruptly turned and looked into John's eyes, John thought he'd never looked into a harder, meaner face. But just as quickly, the man looked down and picked up a hunk of bread.

John got a thick tomato sandwich and a bowl of vegetable soup from Mrs. Miller and sat down next to the guard at a separate table. He wanted to talk about Klein. The guard was eating what looked like stale bread with some lard on it and a piece of cheese.

"Is that all you get?" John couldn't help but ask.

"Got some cold coffee here."

"You have to eat what they eat?" John asked, looking at the PW's food.

"Pretty much. We had a good breakfast, though. Name's Pete. What's yours?"

"John." John didn't know if the guard would find him out of line if he talked about Klein. But he wanted to tell him what he'd seen.

"About that one PW you call Klein. He was standing at that cornfield, maybe three minutes before you found him. He was looking around like he was getting ideas."

"I knew he was there. I could see him."

"Aren't you afraid he's going to escape? I thought he might take off running."

"It occurred to me. But not many men try it. And not on the first day at a new place. If you're gonna escape, you like to have some kind of plan, have some idea where you'll go."

John took a bite of his soup, enjoying it, but feeling a little guilty as he watched the guard tear into the last of his hard bread.

"I've done it," Pete said. "Escaped, that is. I was a PW myself. In Germany. We dug a tunnel and I was one of the lucky ones to make it out." The guard glanced at Klein. "Maybe he's forming a plan, I don't know. But I don't think he'll try to run today."

"He seems different from the other men."

"Yep," Pete nodded. "He's a pro-Nazi type. Not like these other fellows. I'm not sure why he's with these men. They've begun to keep them separate from each other."

"What do you mean? Aren't they all pro-Nazis? They wouldn't be here if they weren't."

"It's not that simple, son. In Germany, if you don't sign up for the military, there's a good chance you'll be killed, or made to do real dangerous work. Men don't have much of a choice. The German army is made up of some men who don't want to be there, and others who believe the war is the only answer to Germany's problems. They think Hitler's the greatest man on Earth. The ones who believe in Hitler don't take kindly to fellow soldiers who don't feel the same way.

"Now Klein, there, he's a dangerous one. He wouldn't think twice about getting rid of a German PW if he thought the man wasn't loyal enough to Hitler. There have been hangings in the prison camps. Those types will gang up on a fellow. That's why we try to keep them in separate quarters. Now some PWs say they're pro-Nazi to protect themselves from soldiers like Klein, but even if these other PWs I brought today would say that, I wouldn't believe them. I've been around these men. They're okay."

John looked at Hans and Fritz, sipping their coffee. He wondered if they had wanted to fight in the war, and how they felt about Hitler. He wondered what he would do if he had to either face death or fight for a cause he didn't believe in.

Sarah approached their table.

"Would you like a sandwich, sir?" she asked Pete, holding out a plate with slices of tomato wedged between thick pieces of homemade bread. "We have an extra."

"Absolutely," Pete said with a grin. "That looks good."

"And my mother was wondering whether it would be all right to make extra food for the PWs tomorrow, unless that's not allowed. Mother says they'll get heartburn eating what they brought today and working all day in the sun."

"That'd be just fine." Pete wiped tomato juice from his chin with the back of his hand. "I know they'd be grateful."

Sarah poured water into a cup for Pete. "You want some more?" she asked John.

"Yes, please."

John watched Sarah work her way down the table. She walked over to Klein, who picked up his cup to hand to Sarah. His hand brushed against hers as she took the cup from his fingers.

Sarah jerked slightly and took a small step backward. But she smiled at Klein as she placed his cup on the table.

"Why is she smiling?" John said irritably, the words popping out before he could stop himself.

"She your girlfriend?" Pete asked.

"No," John said quickly, looking away from Sarah. "I just came here to work. We're hardly even friends." John figured the guard wouldn't believe him, since the color of his face probably matched the tomato Pete was eating.

"Is Klein that PWs first or last name?" John didn't care, but he wanted to change the subject.

"Last. Dieter Klein is his whole name. Don't worry, I'll keep my eye on him."

When Pete went to talk to Mr. Miller, John ran inside to grab his sketchbook. He returned and sat off by himself, looking at Klein, who had gone back to watching the lane. John began to draw. This time he could capture Klein in more detail. He had a small, dark mole on his left cheek and a strong, angular face. He wanted to capture his anger, but didn't know if he could do it.

When he felt the sketch was good enough for the time being, he turned to Hans and Fritz. He squinted his eyes, working out proportions in his head, and began to outline their features. John saw Hans hesitate, taking in the paper and pencil. Their eyes met. Hans tipped his hat and went back to his conversation with Fritz. Other than their clothes, the PWs looked like your average men relaxing on a hot July afternoon. They finished lunch under the shade of a giant weeping willow, under a sky clear and blue as the glass water pitcher in Sarah's hand.

CHAPTER TEN

The next morning John was asked to work with Reuben in the cannery. They were going to make tomato puree. John wasn't exactly sure what tomato puree was, but he was going to find out. "We keep some for ourselves, but most of it is sold to the Campbell Soup Company," Mr. Miller had told him.

John finished eating breakfast and headed outside. It was around seven in the morning, and the dew in the grass made the tips of his shoes damp. The sun was a bright, golden circle, with hazy, reddish-orange lines stretching out in horizontal layers from each side, so pretty that John stood still for a moment, just looking at the painted sky.

He heard Reuben's whistling coming from the cannery and turned his attention toward the odd-looking building that sat near the greenhouses. The Miller farm was well-kept and nice to look at, but the cannery seemed to be made of a combination of cement, wood, and tin. It kind of looked like a lopsided layered wedding cake, with the largest rectangular structure on the bottom, and three additional levels on top, each one narrowing slightly. One side of the building was partially open—large enough for a tractor or two to drive into. There were several pulleys running from the higher floors to the ground level.

Reuben looked up as John entered the building.

"Good morning, John!" he said with a large smile. "Ready to get to work?" He handed him what looked like a large rubber dress.

"You'll be heading to the top floor," Reuben said, "and will want to put that apron on before you begin work. You'll be helping to stir tomatoes in a large vat as they thicken into a puree. It doesn't take a lot of strength to stir the tomatoes, but it does take some stamina."

I'd rather be doing this than catching chickens, John reminded himself a couple of hours later, as he stood stirring what seemed like a swimming pool of steaming tomato juice. The vats were about seven or eight feet tall and five-to-six feet wide. He wore the large rubber apron, which hung down to his ankles. He was so hot that he worried the sweat running down his face would drop into the sauce. He wondered how his body could keep producing so much dripping moisture when he felt parched.

From the fourth floor, John was able to see rows of growing corn stretching out in the distance, and Sarah and the kids working in the garden. If he looked straight down, on the open side of the building, he could see several women at ground level working with crates of tomatoes, feeding each tomato into some kind of machine that pumped them upstairs.

Reuben stood nearby, stirring the other vat. Reuben had either been whistling or singing almost the whole time they worked. He mostly sang church songs. John recognized one or two, but his mother was the only one who went to church every Sunday. John had stopped going when he was around ten, because Pop had stopped. Pop let the boys stay home even though his mom would leave the house with pursed lips, not happy they weren't going along. "You're missing out on being part of the Lord's community," she'd say. "And learning how to be a mindful person." But to John, there was something about a Sunday morning at home that was just as peaceful and spiritual-like as sitting in a church. It was the one time of the week his dad didn't seem to care if he spent his time drawing. John drew, Ben went hiking with Pepper, and his dad read the paper. It was a different kind of quiet—the kind he wished he had moments of every day.

Reuben had a pleasing voice and sounded happy even when he was singing songs about sinners and being downtrodden.

Come home, come home,
You who are weary, come home;
Earnestly, tenderly, Jesus is calling,
Calling, O sinner, come home!

"Do you like to sing?" Reuben asked at the end of a song.

"I don't dislike it, but I don't do it much, either. My mother's the one who sings in my family. She likes to sing to the radio."

"Well, it helps me get through my days," said Reuben. "Good or bad days, I have to sing."

"That's how I feel about my drawings. I like to draw."

"So I've heard. Dorothy showed me the picture you drew of her."

"That picture wasn't finished . . . oh, never mind," John shook his head.

They had just shut down the cannery for the day when Mr. Miller came to tell Reuben he had a couple of visitors waiting. Mr. Miller was grinning.

"I don't know who's here to see me, but it sure has you looking happy," said Reuben.

John walked outside and saw a tan car sitting in the driveway with three men standing by its side. John watched one of the men pat Reuben on the back and hand him the keys. Reuben ran his hand over the hood. He walked around the car and climbed in.

"Well, how about that," said Mrs. Miller as she and Sarah came out of the house to stand beside John.

"What's going on?"

"The church saw fit to buy Reuben and Lydia a car," said Mrs. Miller.

"Why would a church buy him a car?"

"To do the Lord's work. He's their new minister. It's expected he drive from place to place—home visits, the hospital, church meetings, and the like. Reuben's car kept breaking down. He's a good mechanic, but even he couldn't keep that old car running very well with all the miles he's been driving."

John was surprised. Reuben was also a minister? He was so busy at the cannery. Why would he want to work during the week and the weekends? And he didn't really seem like a minister. If he wasn't singing or whistling, he was joking around. And he always wore a baseball cap.

Mrs. Miller went back into the house.

"I still don't get it," said John to Sarah. "Why wouldn't Reuben buy his own car if he needs a new one?"

"He was chosen by the Lord, and the Lord is meeting his needs, John Witmer."

John decided not to ask any more questions. He wondered what Mrs. Miller was making for supper.

CHAPTER ELEVEN

John was so exhausted he overslept in the morning and woke to Sarah pounding on his door. He had to wear the same pants he had on yesterday, and they were filthy. They stank, too. He needed his mom to drop off some more clothes.

"Morning, John!" Reuben called out as John hurried outside and ran to catch up to Reuben as he entered the cannery.

John heard a truck coming down the lane and figured it was the PWs coming to pick tomatoes again.

"I saw you got a new car yesterday," John said.

"Well, it isn't a brand-new car, but it's new to Lydia and me."

"Do churches usually buy their minister a car?"

"Sometimes they do. At my church I don't get paid for the hours I work, and the people are helping us out."

"When did you become a minister?"

"I received the call three weeks ago."

"What does that mean, exactly?" John asked.

"Well, we needed a new minister and the congregation was asked to give names of men they thought would do a good job. Four men were chosen. Our church had a meeting and we four men stood up front. There were four books on a table in front of us. A paper was tucked in one of the books. We each picked a book, and if you got the paper, you became the minister. It's called a 'lot'. I picked the book with the paper in it."

"That's an interesting way to choose a minister," John said. Actually he thought it sounded a little crazy, but didn't say so.

John picked up his apron and headed up the stairs. When Reuben joined him on the top floor, John was stretching to try and work out the stiff muscles he'd gotten from the day before.

Reuben saw him and smiled. "You'll get used to it," he said. John imagined that was true, but by late morning, even with Sarah taking turns with him, his arms and back were aching.

John knew that Mr. Miller hadn't planned on having the PWs help in the cannery because it would make it more difficult for the guard. But after lunch Reuben was called to the hospital to be with a sick church member. Mr. Miller said he needed to use the PWs, and the guard must have said okay because Hans was now stirring the other vat of tomatoes. He had his long sleeves rolled up, but didn't seem to be bothered by the heat. He almost looked like a robot as he stirred with the long wooden spoon, like he could do it for hours.

John jumped at the sound of Hans' voice. "How is your drawing? From lunch, yesterday?"

John looked at him. "Okay, I guess."

"Is that your book over there?"

"Yeah," John said, glancing to where he had his sketchbook setting on top of a box. It was a dumb place to have it, but he thought maybe he'd have a chance to draw again later on. He should have left it in the house.

"May I see it sometime?"

"Why do you want to see it?"

"I liked your drawing of the girl. And I'm curious, especially since you drew a picture of me."

John didn't feel like showing this PW his sketchbook. But he wanted a break from the heat, just for a few seconds, even if it meant calling attention to his work. He decided to show Hans one drawing. He took off his gloves and walked away from the bubbling puree. "You have to look at it over here," he said. "I don't want any tomato juice splashing on it."

Hans walked over and bent down to study the drawing of himself and Fritz. John wondered what he was thinking as he watched Hans lean closer.

"Where did you learn to draw?" Hans asked, as he returned to his vat of tomatoes.

John shrugged. "I just do it."

"No lessons? No advice from anyone?"

"I've never known anyone who could teach me."

I've been around this PW for a couple of days, John thought, *and I'm talking to him about myself—exactly what I predicted Sarah would be doing. But stirring tomatoes gets pretty boring after awhile, and what is the harm in talking about art?*

"When you're older, maybe you'll have a chance to study somewhere," Hans continued. "When I said you were good before, I did not lie. I have never seen anyone so young draw people the way you do—quickly and yet with layers of detail, of emotion. You should not waste such talent."

John watched the bubbling tomato sauce. No one in his family had ever told him he shouldn't let his talent go to waste, or that when he was older he should study art somewhere.

"It's not worth much, being able to draw," John said. John's dad had said that many times. He didn't know why he'd said it out loud now, to a PW. Had he actually come to believe it too?

"Why do you say that?" Hans asked.

"Hard to make a living at it."

"It can be difficult, yes. But not impossible. And you may not become rich." Hans took his hat off and ran his hand over his whitish-blond hair. He actually looked a bit warm now.

John stared at Hans, willing Hans to look him in the eyes. "How do you know? And what makes you think my work is anything special? How do you know what's good?"

Hans stared back, his blue eyes confident. "I was a painter. In Berlin. I studied two years at university before I joined the army. But I had lessons for many years before that from my father. He is also an artist, and many of his friends. He owned a gallery."

John couldn't believe it. He'd never met anyone who really knew anything about art. "Could he make a living like that? Showing paintings in a gallery?"

"Sometimes he drew illustrations for books," Hans said, almost speaking in time to the movement of his arm, stirring the tomatoes. "But the gallery was successful, and he was known for his landscapes. We had so many in our house."

Hans grew quiet. John knew that feeling, when a memory enveloped you, wrapping you in sadness, making you close in on yourself.

John circled the long wooden spoon around and around. The sound of it occasionally bumping the side of the vat competed with the silence that seemed to stretch for endless minutes. Hans surprised him when he abruptly turned and asked, "So, what do you want to do? With your art?"

John had never told anyone about his dream. It felt strange, but good, to say it out loud. "There's an art school in Philadelphia I've read about. Not that far from here. I'd go there after high school if I could. They have some scholarships for people who can't afford it. That would be me for sure."

"That's good to look at schools."

"Except my father won't want me to go. He expects me to work with him, in his woodshop. He thinks it would be a big waste of time and money to go away to study art. He says I already know how to draw, anyway."

Hans smiled. "You do. But there is always more to learn. Sometime I'll show you a trick or two. If you'd like."

John heard footsteps and bit back his eager reply.

Fritz came up the steps and spoke to Hans.

"You can take a break," Hans said to John. "Fritz says the pretty girl wants you. She's waiting outside."

John glanced at Fritz, who gave him a wink and nodded in the direction of the house.

Looking outside, John saw the rest of the PWs standing in a line, though with a fair bit of distance between them. Cans traveled down a pulley to where the first man was waiting, wearing thick gloves. He picked up a hot can as it came rolling off the track and threw it to the fellow behind him. That PW then threw it eight or ten feet to another man standing behind him. Klein was last in line, stacking the cans to cool. Pete stood nearby, his rifle held loosely by his side.

Sarah was standing by a tree several feet away from the men, smiling at John and waving excitedly. What did Sarah need him for and why did she have to make a scene?

Reuben must have returned, as John heard his voice as he went down the creaky, ladder-type wooden stairs to the first floor. From saying prayers at a deathbed to running a cannery—that was a full day, John thought. Klein had finished stacking cans and stood with Reuben near the boiler. John knew the boiler had to be maintained to keep the stoves hot upstairs, but he hoped Reuben wasn't teaching Klein to do it. John didn't trust him farther than he could spit.

Sarah rushed toward him as soon as he stepped outside.

"John! Jake just got back from town and bumped into your mother. She had a letter from your father and gave it to him."

Sarah held out a brown envelope, which John reached for in disbelief. John knew his father had not touched this envelope himself. The military took pictures of the soldiers' letters and sent the rolls of film to the United States to save money. Inside the envelope would be a picture of his dad's letter, which had been printed in the US. John was stunned to see his name through the oval window. His father never wrote to him directly.

John ran his fingers along the envelope.

"Aren't you going to read it?" Sarah asked impatiently.

John hesitated, then tucked the envelope into his back pants pocket. "Yeah. But later. When I'm done working." *And when I'm alone*, he thought. He couldn't imagine what his dad was writing to him about, and he didn't want anyone watching him while he read it.

Sarah looked surprised. "Suit yourself."

John turned to walk back to the cannery. The men were now stacking the cans of tomato sauce in boxes. No one stood by the boiler. John began to climb up the stairs. His foot had just hit the top floor when a loud hissing sound, then a cracking explosion, made the wooden floor vibrate beneath his feet.

"John! Hans! Fritz!" Reuben hollered. "Come down!" "*Komm schnell runter!*"

John turned to see Hans and Fritz hurrying toward him. John started down the long ladder, going as fast as he could. He had just passed the second floor, when Reuben jumped back from the boiler as another loud crack rocked the building. The explosion shook the ladder as John's foot reached for the next rung. His foot missed. He tried to hold on, grabbing wildly at the ladder, but he was falling backward, too fast and too forcefully to get a grip.

John landed hard on his side, his head slamming onto the wooden floor. He lay still, trying to adjust to the pain. What were those smells? Burning rubber? Smoke? Pushing himself up slowly with his hands, he saw men trying to fight flames with some blankets and stomping their feet.

"John!" Reuben called. "Hans! Fritz! Head back upstairs! You're surrounded! You'll have to jump!"

John tried to stand, but his legs buckled under him. He couldn't focus. He could feel the heat of the fire now, hear its crackling dance. Maybe if he rolled . . .

"John, no!" Reuben yelled.

Hands yanked at the back of John's shirt. Someone was grabbing at his leg, wrapping something around it, smothering flames. It hurt like nothing he'd ever felt before. Was that his voice screaming? German words were yelled into his ear as he was picked up and hoisted over someone's shoulder. He felt himself being carried, his leg bumping against the stairs.

"We have to throw you," a blurry face said, hovering above him.

John felt himself being rocked backwards.

"*Pass auf!*" a voice yelled. And he was flying

CHAPTER TWELVE

"Jake! Call Dr. Fisher's office. See if he can come out here. Tell him we got a couple of boys who need attention, and one's a PW."

"John? John, can you hear me?"

John heard voices from far off. Urgent in tone. Calling his name. He felt like his head was floating gently, slowly, in a dark place he couldn't touch, didn't recognize. Yet, there was pain too. Searing pain. Like a million fire ants were attacking his leg.

"His eyelids are moving."

"Dorothy, move back. You'll accidentally bump him."

"You're just as close to him as me, Sarah."

John laid still. He recognized the voices now. He didn't know where he was, but figured if Sarah and Dorothy were bickering, he was at least still alive and on Earth.

"Both you girls get back now! Sarah, take Dorothy inside and get some water for John. Then keep an eye on him. I have to help the men."

John had never heard Mr. Miller sound angry before. He rested, willing his head to clear, and slowly opened his eyes. Sarah was walking toward him, once again carrying cups and the blue pitcher.

"John!" she leaned over him. "How do you feel?"

John tried to speak, but it took so much effort. He closed his eyes again. His head was pounding. His stomach was nauseous. And his leg. It was throbbing. Excruciating pain that was getting worse with each second. Something was touching it and he couldn't stand it.

"John?"

"My leg . . ." His voice was raspy, barely sounding like his own.

"You fell from the steps and your pant leg caught fire. You got burned some around your ankle and calf. We called the doctor."

John didn't remember anything but the noise and falling from the steps.

Reuben and Jake ran past, pulling a hose. "Turn the water on!" Reuben yelled.

"You want some water to drink?" Sarah held up a glass. "I brought some out."

John nodded and began to sit up. It was hard to breathe—he felt like the fire had reached his lungs, like they were still burning. Sarah's face began to weave before his eyes.

"Easy." Sarah took his arm and pulled him up slowly. "Here." She handed him a cup. "Can you hold it?"

"Yes," he said, but his hand shook as he reached for the cup.

"Just drink." Sarah moved the cup to his lips. "I'll hold it."

"I can do it."

"Drink." She tipped water into his mouth.

John felt the water slide down his throat. It was ice cold. He put his hand over Sarah's, to tip the cup upward again. It was so good, he couldn't get enough.

"That's it boys! We got it!" Mr. Miller's voice yelled out.

"Thank goodness," Sarah said. "I thought we might lose the whole cannery."

"How did I get out of there?" John lay back on the grass and shielded his eyes against the bright sun. "I can't remember anything."

"Hans and Fritz tossed you right down from the second floor, and Jake caught you. Here they all come now."

John watched the men walk slowly out of the cannery. Mr. Miller and Hans headed toward them.

"Sit here, Hans," Mr. Miller said. "The doctor should be here soon. I'll find you a spare shirt."

Hans glanced at John. "Are you all right?"

"I guess so."

"How's your leg?"

"Hurts." John noticed some reddish patches on Hans' arm. "Did you get burned too?"

"A little."

"Did your shirt burn right off you or what?"

"My shirt is wrapped around your ankle."

John glanced at his leg. He hadn't noticed that the blue cloth tied around his ankle was a PW work shirt.

"I used it to put the fire out." Hans drank the cup of water Sarah had given him, and then leaned back, closing his eyes.

John stared at the muscular man lying next to him. Sweat glistened on his bare chest. Black soot was streaked across his cheek, but he was still wearing his hat. Red burn marks checkered his right arm, the hair singed right off. John knew how that hurt. He tried to memorize the face and the posture of this man who had helped save him. He'd try to draw the picture later.

His sketchbook! He remembered taking it to the cannery. "My sketchbook!" he said out loud, his voice hoarse but panicked. "It's in . . ."

"I found it and tossed it down to her—Sarah," Hans murmured. "It should be all right."

"Thanks." John felt like his heart was jumping out of his chest. "Thanks a lot." John knew his words were inadequate. But what could he say? It hurt to talk anyway.

Hans gave a slight nod of his head. He sat up and looked at Sarah. "Do you think there will be work tomorrow?"

"There will be tomatoes to pick. I don't know what shape the cannery will be in."

They looked at the smoking building. Only the first floor looked damaged. John figured something had gone wrong with the boiler, and was amazed the whole thing hadn't blown up.

The men had turned away from the building, some helping Reuben pull the long hose as they walked. Pete trailed behind, somehow having managed to hang on to his rifle even though he had helped to put out the fire. Pete stopped and glanced over his shoulder.

"Where's Klein?" he barked.

The men shrugged.

"Anyone seen Klein?" he yelled.

"I saw him maybe five, ten minutes ago," Reuben said. "On the grass over there, watching."

"Son of a . . . Tell the men to sit down and stay down!" he said to Reuben. "Yell if they move. He couldn't have gotten far."

CHAPTER THIRTEEN

Mrs. Miller began to carefully peel off the shirt wrapped around John's leg. Part of it stuck to a raw patch of skin.

"Ahh!" John yelled. He thought he had felt the worst, was prepared to take what was coming, but the pain kept surprising him.

"This will protect the burn until the doctor treats it," Mrs. Miller squeezed aloe from a plant onto his burned ankle.

John nodded, but he must have looked skeptical.

"Don't worry, I've done this before," Mrs. Miller said. "My grandmother was known for her home remedies. This was one of the first things she taught me."

John had to admit the thick liquid felt better on his leg than the rough material that had been touching his skin. He looked at the raw, red flesh around his calf. It was already beginning to blister.

Mrs. Miller had insisted they come inside, not wanting any dirt to get into the aloe. He and Hans were sitting at the kitchen table. The white curtains framing the open windows looked like they were breathing, moving in and out with the slight breeze.

Jake and Mr. Miller were out helping to look for Klein. Every sound on the farm seemed magnified now. Leaves rustling, a door slamming. Even the silence was filled with expectation. Waiting. Wondering.

Mrs. Miller began to treat Hans's arm. "This doesn't look too bad," she said. "Though I know it still hurts."

Hans was looking at some artwork hanging on the wall. "Your parents?" he asked, nodding at the names written in decorative Old English calligraphy, surrounded by painted flowers. At the top it said, "Family Record."

"Yes." Mrs. Miller pointed at the names. "My parents and my siblings. I'm right in the middle there. We had one done for Elam's family also. But I've yet to get one made with my own children."

"This is a . . . what is the word . . . tradition?"

"Yes, I guess you could say that. Our Amish neighbor makes them. Amish don't do much in the way of decorating their homes. But they all have family records like this. We Mennonites seem to like them too."

"I learned how to write a bit like that when I was at a prison camp, in Colorado," Hans said with a slight smile. "They had some classes we could take. I was surprised at some of the choices."

"You could take classes? In a prison camp?" John asked.

"Yes. I think most of the camps offer something. In Missouri I studied European history. We had good soccer tournaments there as well. We went to work during the day, but there was time in the evening for other things."

"Why?" asked John. "Why would they let you do those things?"

"Why?" repeated Hans. "I guess to show us America is a good country. To show us how your democracy works. To make us think better of your country and question our own. And I think they want American POWs to be treated well in Germany. But I don't believe the Americans will be treated like we have been. Hitler does not think like your Roosevelt."

Mr. Miller walked into the kitchen. "We can't find him," he said, looking at Mrs. Miller. "Keep the children in the house. I have to call the sheriff."

John could hear Sarah in the living room, playing a board game with Dorothy and Kenny. The neighbor children had been taken home.

"I'm sorry for the trouble with Klein," Hans said. "The rest of us like working here. Very much."

"I'm glad to hear it," said Mrs. Miller, "because we need the workers. I'm not sure what will happen after this."

Mrs. Miller set a plate of cookies on the table. "These cookies don't have the right amount of sugar in them, with the rations and all. But the children say they're still good. Help yourselves."

John didn't feel like he could eat. The pain in his leg was so intense it was all he could think about, all he could focus on. He felt himself start to slump forward.

"Doctor Thompson's here!" Jake called out as he stepped into the kitchen, followed by a thin, white-haired man. Jake stomped his feet on the floor mat. "And Hans, you're to come with me. Pete's taking you guys back to the camp, after the sheriff gets here."

Each stomp of Jake's feet sent tremors through John's leg. His forehead rested on his arms, folded on the table. His eyes watered, but he couldn't stand the thought of crying. He could take this. He had to. Hans didn't even act like he was in much pain.

"Come in, come in," said Mrs. Miller. "Jake, help me carry John to the sofa—or should we carry him up to his bed, Dr. Thompson?"

"Let's carry him to his bed. I can see from here he needs a shot of morphine, which is going to make him sleepy. I'll give this PW a shot too before he leaves, and bandage up his arm. I assume there will be a doctor that can keep an eye on this at the prison camp?"

"Yes, sir," Hans said.

John wanted to say good-bye to Hans. He figured he'd never see him again. But Mrs. Miller and Jake were picking him up and everyone seemed to be talking at once. He had to close his eyes, as once again a sweeping blackness was creeping in to claim him.

"He'll be all right," he heard the doctor say. "He seems to be in a bit of shock. And he's got at least a second-degree burn here. That's about as painful as it comes. So Anna Miller, when's the last time you gave a shot?"

CHAPTER FOURTEEN

John awoke with a start. He felt something soft on his hand. Sarah sat back quickly in her chair beside the bed. Had she been holding his hand?

"How are you?" she asked. "Mother sent me to check on you."

"Drowsy. But better. The morphine works pretty good."

Sarah smiled. "Mother will give you another shot when you need it."

"She told me her grandmother taught her healing, or something like that."

Sarah laughed. "Don't worry. Mother was a nurse before she got married. She knows what she's doing."

Sarah leaned closer to the bed. "John, the sheriff wants to talk to you. Is it all right to get him?"

"Why? I didn't see anything. I can't even remember things that happened to me."

"Then it won't take long," Sarah said, getting up. "I'll be right back."

John looked out of the window. It was still light outside, so he hadn't slept too long. He guessed Klein was still on the run, or the sheriff wouldn't need to talk to him. John couldn't imagine Klein trying to stay hidden here on the farm, but you never knew.

A man stepped through the door, Mr. Miller and Sarah behind him. "John, the sheriff is going to ask you a few questions," Mr. Miller said.

John watched the sheriff walk closer to his bed. He hoped the sheriff wouldn't have to actually run after Klein, because he had a noticeable stomach pouch hanging over his belt, and John wouldn't be surprised if Klein had won a few races in his day.

"This will be quick. I'm just wondering if you saw or heard anything from the runaway PW you think might help us in our search?" The sheriff glanced at John's ankle as he spoke, which was covered with aloe.

"No sir. I can't think of anything."

John knew describing Klein standing at the edge of the cornfield wouldn't help. Neither would saying that he suspected Klein started the fire. John hadn't seen him do anything, and it would make Pete and the Millers look bad.

"Well, that's what I figured," the sheriff said, "but I wanted to check with everybody who was around. So we've got a man in blue PW work clothes, with short, dark hair, over six feet tall. Not much to go on, but we'll find him."

"John, you drew a picture of Klein," Sarah said, excitement in her voice. "When we were eating! Maybe that would help the sheriff."

The sheriff looked at John. "I don't know. Think it'd be good enough to actually help?"

"If John drew it, it's good enough," Sarah said.

"Don't they have a photograph of him at the prison camp or something?" John asked. "That would probably be more useful."

"There's some kind of mix-up," the sheriff answered, shaking his head. "The photo they have under his name is of some blond fellow. Doesn't match his description at all. They're trying to sort it out. But in the meantime I'll take a look at your drawing."

Why couldn't Sarah keep her mouth closed? He didn't want to give away his drawing of Klein to this man. The sheriff would probably ball it up and toss it out if he didn't think it would help him. John wanted to help find Klein, but he wasn't sure this was the way to do it. He was possessive of his drawings, and a little self conscious about showing them to strangers. He always had been.

"I'll get it for him, John. I put your sketchbook in the desk over there." Sarah said.

"Just hand it to me." John was furious with Sarah, but had to act like he wasn't with Mr. Miller and the sheriff watching him. But no way was Sarah going to look through all of his drawings in front of these men.

John carefully pulled out the sketch of Klein sitting at the picnic table and handed it to the sheriff.

"This look like him?" the sheriff asked Mr. Miller.

"That's him. Nice-looking fellow, but he always had a sour look on his face. Just like that."

"All right then. I'll take this with me." The sheriff slapped the drawing against his leg a couple of times as he walked toward the door.

"What do you think your Amish neighbors would do if this PW showed up at their place?" he stopped and asked.

"I couldn't say for sure," Mr. Miller answered. "They might feed him if he asked for food, but they wouldn't hide him."

"Sure about that? They might feel inclined to help him, being against war, and the PW being German and all."

"The Amish wouldn't want an escaped prisoner of war hanging around their farm."

"What about you? You seem friendly enough with these German prisoners. Where do you stand on the war?"

"I wouldn't help a PW escape, if that's what you're asking. This fellow has an edge to him. I believe he might be a dangerous man. I don't relish the thought of him wandering about, close to my family."

The sheriff looked at Mr. Miller and nodded. "The FBI has already been called. We'll find him."

CHAPTER FIFTEEN

July 1944
Fort Indiantown Gap, Pennsylvania
Prisoner of War Camp

"You think Klein started the fire?" Fritz asked.

Hans nodded. "I don't know what he did to cause the explosion, but he did something."

"He used to be an engineer," Wilheim said. "It wouldn't be hard for him to cause trouble."

"I didn't know that." Hans shook his head. "I liked working on that farm. I want to go back. It's the best work assignment I've had in this country."

Wilheim touched his swollen nose. "I told them I was ready to work so I could go to this farm. I was scheduled to go with you tomorrow. Now I'll probably get a new assignment."

"We don't know for sure that we're not going back," Hans said.

Fritz looked around the dining hall for a moment, listening to the hum of conversations. No one seemed to be paying attention to them. "Where do you think Klein escaped to? I couldn't believe he got away."

Hans shrugged. "Who knows? I'm glad he's gone."

"He'll be caught," Wilheim said. "He's too sure of himself. He'll do something to make someone notice him."

"I think he just wants a woman." Fritz grinned. "Who doesn't? Did you see the way he watched the girl at the farm?"

"You think he's hiding at the farm to be near this girl?" Wilheim asked.

"He wouldn't be that stupid," Hans said. "For one, she's too young for him. Two, did you forget he tried to blow up their building? He would run far from that place."

Fritz shook his head. "I don't know. He does what he wants. She's beautiful and his eyes followed her as if he thought she was old enough."

"How old is this girl?" asked Wilheim.

"She looks about sixteen." Fritz looked at Wilhelm. "I know I haven't seen many females over the last couple of years, but this girl is one of the most stunning girls I've ever seen. It's almost strange when you first notice her, like maybe you're not seeing right."

"She looks older, but she's thirteen, not sixteen, and an innocent farm girl," said Hans. "The little girl, Dorothy, told me how old they all were. Klein would do better putting distance between himself and the farm. I hate to admit it, but he is good-looking enough to find a lonely woman somewhere along the way who will pay attention to him."

"I hope he's that smart," said Fritz. "I hope he's gone."

CHAPTER SIXTEEN

John stared at the ceiling. He couldn't sleep. He couldn't read. He couldn't even draw. The morphine was wearing off and the raw, harrowing pain was excruciating and relentless. He was sweating, but shivering—sure signs of a fever.

And though he was exhausted, thoughts thrashed around in his mind. What had started the fire, or who? Where was Klein? Was he causing someone harm? Could John work on the Miller farm anymore? Would the other PWs come back? Did he actually want them to?

Mrs. Miller had said to wake her if he needed help, and had put a bell by the bed. But waking the whole household up at four in the morning didn't seem right. He figured the bedrooms were close together and everyone would hear the bell. Maybe he should have gone home. It would have been just him and his mom and Pepper. His mom wasn't a nurse, but she would have fussed over him. And at least he could listen to the radio at home. Listening to the adventures of "The Lone Ranger" or hearing "The Shadow" tell a creepy detective story would have helped keep his mind off the aching in his leg.

He wondered what his dad was doing right now—if he was sleeping or fighting. He felt like he could empathize with the soldiers just a little bit tonight, being in pain like he was. But he couldn't imagine what a gunshot wound would feel like, or getting your arm or leg torn off.

John shook his head. He didn't want to think about these things. But something was eating at him, other than the pain.

John tried to think back to the fire. Why had he been on the stairs anyway?

Sarah. He had been talking to Sarah. And she'd given him a letter from Pop. John jerked himself upright. He'd put it in a pocket. How could he have forgotten? What if he had lost it? What if it had fallen out of his pocket and burned?

He had been wearing his brown pants. He was now just in his underwear. How had that happened?

John glanced around the room. It was too dark to see anything.

He pushed the sheet away and swung his legs around to the side of the bed. He gripped the headboard and sucked in his stomach to keep from crying out when he bumped his ankle. The morphine had taken away his headache, but he was so groggy. He waited for the room to stop sliding around and stand still.

Jake had crutches on hand from a time when he'd broken a leg. They now rested by the side of the bed. John grabbed them and slowly made his way to the light switch. Mrs. Miller had cut the bottom section of his one pant leg off to treat his burn. Would she have thrown the pants away?

What if the letter had fallen out of his pocket and was lying in the cannery somewhere, or on the lawn? If it rained, the letter would be ruined. John made his way to the window. It was dark out, but the moon cast a pale light on the grass and the glass of the greenhouses. He saw a flicker of movement by the edge of the chicken shed and felt goose bumps rise on his arms. Had someone just walked around the building? John watched for a few more minutes. The wind was probably just blowing a bush around.

John wondered if he would have the nerve to roam around out there if he were healthy. He didn't think Klein would have stayed on the farm, but then again, Klein knew a bit about the farm, and where he could hide. Any of the greenhouses would work. John wondered if he would have risked meeting up with Klein in order to find his dad's letter. He liked to think so.

John pushed his bangs out of his eyes. He saw something green on the chair, which was pushed under the desk. His shirt? He pulled out the chair. Underneath the shirt were his pants. Burned, but folded neatly. John found the back pocket and his fingers touched paper.

John hobbled over to the bed. With shaking hands, he carefully pulled out two sheets of folded paper, opened the first, and began to read.

June 8, 1944

Dear John,

How are you, son? I hope you're helping your mother as best you can. I'll be glad when this war's over and I can come home to all of you.

Last evening, when things were quieting down, the combat artist who stays with us was on deck finishing up a painting. I was going to join some guys on the ship for a game of cards, but Al said he would draw me alone if I wanted him to. Believe it or not, I stood still so a man could draw a picture of me. Watching him work always reminds me of you, and I thought you might like to have this drawing of me. I don't know if he's supposed to, but Al sometimes draws a quick picture of a soldier, and gives it to him so he can send it home.

I imagine you've heard of combat artists, and have already seen some of their pictures in that *Life* magazine your mother insists on getting. I don't know if I understand the need for these combat artists, though. Why have someone in a foxhole, looking out to draw our soldiers being torn up, when they could be fighting? But I guess they capture what we're going through, for those who want to see it.

Sadly, all those men who were playing cards are dead. The ship was hit. Me and Al managed to escape unharmed. I don't know why I was spared, with barely a scratch, but here's the drawing that saved my life.

Pop

John laid the letter down on the bed and opened the second sheet of paper. He could hardly believe his eyes.

There was his dad, in his helmet, standing tall and straight, holding his rifle by his side. He looked like he was thinking hard about something. John smiled. That was typical of Pop, always so serious. It was a simple pencil drawing, yet John felt it captured the quiet intensity of his dad's personality. His eyes looked hard, weary, yet still had life in them. He wasn't beaten yet. John had heard of men coming home who acted half-crazy. People said the war had warped their minds. John could tell his dad knew what he was about, just from that drawing. How had the artist done that, with a few swipes of a pencil?

John felt determined he would be that good someday. Be able to show a man's mind on paper. He wondered if his dad would be more open to him studying art after being around combat artists.

John opened his sketchpad. His leg was still throbbing, but he tried to ignore it as he began to sketch an outline of Hans, lying on the grass after the fire. He couldn't draw men in combat, but he could capture another side of the war. Maybe his dad would like to see these drawings when he came home.

CHAPTER SEVENTEEN

John split open a pea pod and shook five peas into the bowl on his lap. It was the second morning after the fire. Yesterday, Mrs. Miller had insisted that John stay in bed all day, but today when he woke up and saw the bright morning light coming through the window, he decided he had to feel the sun on his face. It had taken him twenty minutes to make it from the bedroom to the porch. Going down a winding, curving staircase with crutches, a sketchpad, a burned leg, and on morphine probably hadn't been a smart idea, as he'd almost fallen several times. His book had slipped out of his hand and tumbled down a couple of stairs, too. But in spite of everything, including Sarah's and Mrs. Miller's scolding, he was happy to be sitting outside.

"Any word about that Dieter Klein?" he asked Sarah.

"Nope. Not a thing. And the sheriff wants to find him in the worst way. I heard him talking to my dad this morning. They've been searching everywhere, but haven't found one clue where he could be. The FBI are looking too, but the sheriff would love to find him first. He didn't say that exactly, but I could tell. Kept saying him being local and all, he should know where to look."

John shifted in the hard wooden chair. When he'd come outside, Sarah had been sitting on the porch shelling peas, and John thought he should help her. But her fingers were so quick, she shelled about five pods to his one.

John looked up as the door to a greenhouse opened. Mr. Miller walked out, followed by Hans. They headed toward the house.

"Hans came back?" John felt like it shouldn't matter to him, but he was relieved to see him.

"All of them came back, and a new man named Wilhelm to replace the runaway one. My dad was so glad when Jake showed up with them yesterday.

Dad thought Jake might return with an empty truck because of the fire and all."

"John, Sarah," Mr. Miller said as he walked up the porch stairs. "Hans is going to join you here for a little while. He's not complaining, but I believe he needs a rest. Also, your mother has a special job for him," he told Sarah.

Hans nodded at John and Sarah, and then looked back at Mr. Miller. "I can work. Wherever you need me."

John saw Pete take a step out of the greenhouse and look toward the porch. He stayed outside, watching the PWs in the greenhouse through the glass windows, and keeping an eye on Hans at the same time. John wondered if Pete had gotten in trouble for Klein's escape.

"Wait here," Mr. Miller said to Hans, and went into the house.

Hans had a bandage around his arm, and John thought he looked pale and tired.

"Does your arm hurt much?" John asked.

"It's not a problem," Hans answered, but he coughed after he spoke.

"John has been coughing a lot too," Sarah said. "The doctor said it's from breathing in so much smoke, but it should go away in a few days."

"Do you have a burning feeling in your lungs?" John asked Hans.

"Yes, a little."

Mr. Miller returned with a card table and a couple of Bibles. He looked at Hans. "I hope you won't mind using that fancy writing Anna says you know. She'd like some names written in these Bibles."

Surprise flashed across Hans's face. "Are you sure you want me writing in your Bibles?"

"Oh, yes. My wife has wanted this done for some time now. We just didn't have anyone to do it."

Hans stepped forward. He picked up an ancient-looking calligraphy pen and shook the bottle of black ink. "I'll try."

"Anna tucked the names you are to write inside the Bibles. Just rewrite them in ink on the inside cover here. I'll be in the office for a bit. If you finish before I get back, stay here with John and Sarah. I won't be long."

Mr. Miller gave Sarah and John a look. John figured that meant don't go anywhere, stay here with Hans.

John kept shelling peas until his curiosity got the better of him. He worked his way over to the card table and watched Hans slowly write "Sarah Fern Miller."

Hans finished and glanced up, taking in the loose bandage wrapped around John's lower leg. "How is it?"

"Okay." John shifted his weight on his crutches to get more comfortable. He gave Hans a pained smile. "Well, to be honest, it hurts like crazy. It never stops."

Hans nodded. "Maybe you should sit."

John wondered if Hans could see his eyes glazing over. Because they were. He was beginning to see double. Sarah now had four hands flying over the peas.

John moved back to his chair. "Yeah, the morphine makes me feel a little strange. I get dizzy when I stand."

"I know. They gave me some last night, but I refused it this morning. I couldn't work if I took it."

Dorothy came out of the house and walked over to Hans. "What are you doing?"

"I'm going to write your name in this Bible."

"Why?"

"Your father asked me to."

John's vision cleared, and he picked up his sketchbook. He drew Dorothy standing close to the table, biting her lip as she watched, and Hans, with his hat resting in his lap, bent over the Bible, his forehead slightly wrinkled in concentration.

"Is that hard?" Dorothy asked as Hans sat back in his chair.

"It just takes practice. You hold the pen like this, at an angle. Then bring the pen down." Hans handed Dorothy the calligraphy pen and a piece of scrap paper he had practiced on. "Try it," he said.

Dorothy scraped the pen along the paper. "Nothing happened."

"Here," Hans put his hand around Dorothy's. "Relax your hand and we'll write a letter 'D' together."

Dorothy wrote the rest of her name.

"My letters don't look like yours. They're all messy."

"It takes practice. Your letters are better than mine were when I first tried this."

"Really?"

"Absolutely."

"Come help with the peas, Dorothy," Sarah said. "Let Hans get back to his work."

John was still sketching when Hans cleaned off the pen and stood up.

"Since you have to wait for Mr. Miller, do you feel like looking at my book?" John asked. "You said you could maybe offer me some tips some time." John didn't know if his request was appropriate, but he decided he'd ask. When would be a good time to ask a PW for an art lesson, anyway?

Hans held out his hand for the sketchbook. He leafed through the pages, ending with the drawing of himself and Dorothy. "I'm amazed at how quickly you draw faces," he said. "And you see the little details. This is quite good, but perhaps you could experiment with some . . . I don't know how to say it in English. But look . . ."

Hans crouched down by John's chair. "Look what happens when I draw short lines like this, and now the other way, on her shoulder. You make . . . what is the word . . . texture. And if you smudge this a bit here, you will create a softer shadow on her face." Hans passed the book back to John.

John nodded. "I see what you mean. Thanks."

John heard the rumble of a truck, then the cut of the engine. He looked up to see Jake hop from the front seat, and grin when he caught John's eye.

"You'll never believe it," he said, as he approached the porch.

"What?" Sarah asked. But Jake was looking at John.

"Look at this," he said, as he held up the front page of the newspaper.

The headline read, "Escaped POW still on the loose in Lancaster County." Underneath was John's drawing of Klein.

CHAPTER EIGHTEEN

"Ever had your name in the newspaper before?" asked Jake. "Listen to this: 'Local boy, John Witmer, drew the picture of the POW when working on the farm of Elam Miller. The POW, Dieter Klein, escaped from the Miller farm while on work duty. When the sheriff asked Miller if the drawing resembled the escaped man, Miller said, 'That's him. He always had a sour look on his face.'"

"Dad's not going to like that," Sarah said. "I think they changed his words somehow."

"They never said anything about printing it in the newspaper," John said.

Jake shrugged. "I guess they figure they'll do what they want since they're trying to catch an escaped PW. It is something, isn't it? That your picture might help catch him?"

John shrugged. "Klein's no good. If my drawing helps catch him, I'm glad I gave it." John glanced at Hans, who was standing near the table. John knew Hans and Klein weren't friendly, but he wondered if Hans hoped Klein would remain free, if he would automatically want a fellow prisoner to thwart the Americans.

Hans took a step forward. "May I see it?" he asked Jake.

"Guess so," Jake answered, and handed him the paper.

Hans studied the drawing. "You even drew this," he said to John with a slight smile, pointing to the side of his mouth.

"It's called a mole," John said.

"Klein would not imagine you being able to cause him this trouble," Hans said.

John sat on the porch after everyone left. He watched Hans walk back to the greenhouse with Mr. Miller. Sarah had been right. Her dad had not been pleased when he read the paper. He didn't like the quote, or having his name and farm mentioned. The reporter even wrote about the fire. John knew how Mr. Miller felt. John didn't like having his drawing and his name in the paper either. Klein was still out there. What if he saw the picture and John's name? Would he come after him somehow? Max bounded up the steps and ran over to John's chair, his tail wagging.

"Don't jump on my sore leg, Max." John snapped his fingers. "Sit." Max seemed to understand and sat by John's good leg. John smoothed down the soft, straight fur. He didn't usually pay too much attention to Max. He couldn't pet him without thinking of his own dog, and worrying about how he was doing without anyone to talk to him. His mom would feed Pepper, but that was about it.

But at this moment, as he stroked Max's head and looked out at the sun lighting up the green grass across the wide yard, and took in Mrs. Miller's red geraniums planted in clusters here and there, he could almost convince himself life was peaceful and normal. The heat felt still and comforting, like an invisible blanket layered over him as he leaned his head back and closed his eyes.

"Excuse me? Hello?"

John jumped. He must have been sleeping, because he had no sense of time or place. He looked up at a man hovering over him, staring at his face. John had never seen him before. John looked down at Max, who hadn't made a sound.

"Not a great watch dog, is he?" the man asked with a smile.

"Guess not. He isn't mine." John pushed his chair back, not liking the man standing so close to him.

"Can I help you with something?"

"Are you John? John Witmer?"

"Yes. Who are you?"

"Mark Burnes. Nice to meet you." Mark stuck his hand out.

John leaned forward and grasped the moist hand of the smiling stranger. He had blond, wispy hair and light brown eyes. John thought he'd look a lot better without his poor excuse of a mustache. He looked like he was in his mid-twenties, but the few, thin hairs struggling to grow over his upper lip just made him look like he was playing at being an adult.

"I'm with the newspaper, and I'd like to ask you a few questions. People are curious about the boy who drew the escaped POW. I'd like to run a little feature story on you, and why you drew that picture to begin with."

Burnes took out a tablet and a pen. "That all right with you?" he asked, but quickly followed with his next question without waiting for John to reply.

"So John, when did you begin drawing?"

John stared at Burnes. He wondered if Mr. Miller would like this man on his farm, asking questions.

"I don't really want an article written about me."

"Are you kidding? Most people like to enjoy a moment of fame when they get a chance. Enjoy the attention, John. People are going to give it to you."

"People are interested in Klein, not me," John said.

"So what was Klein like? Did you talk to him? How did he feel about that picture you drew of him?"

"He didn't speak English. And I didn't show him the drawing."

Burnes' fingers flew across his tablet. John wondered how he was finding so much to write about, when he was barely answering his questions.

"So tell me about yourself, John. Believe me, people are going to want to know about the boy who helped capture an escaped POW. You do know they caught him, don't you?"

John sat up straighter. "They caught him? Where? When?"

Burnes laughed. "See what I mean? You're full of questions. I'm being asked questions too. Who was the boy who drew the picture? Why did he draw it? Did he know the POW? See what I mean? And to answer your question, they caught him about ten miles south of here. Only about an hour after the paper came out. A waitress recognized him when he walked into a diner with a woman and called the sheriff. He was in civilian clothes, but she'd just seen the newspaper and recognized him, no problem."

John stared at the reporter. He couldn't believe it. His drawing had actually helped.

"You look surprised. Didn't you have any faith in your drawing?"

"Someone still had to see him."

The reporter scribbled in his tablet.

"So John, tell me, where were you when you drew that picture?"

"Sitting. At a picnic table. But I don't want an article written about me."

"John, my editor will insist upon it. If you don't want to be interviewed, I'll ask some other folks around the farm. This could be a good thing for you, if you'd work with me. You're obviously a very talented boy. Where did you learn to draw like that?"

John knew he wasn't going to win. This man would write an article. He thought of his dad. He'd save it for him. Maybe it would make him proud that he used his art for a good purpose, that he helped capture Klein.

"I just do it."

"Why did you draw Klein?"

"I don't know. I had paper. I looked at him and started drawing. I'm always drawing. Whenever I can, anyway. I can't tell you I had a feeling I would need the drawing for anything. I just did it."

"John, what if I told you the paper was going to sponsor an art contest for drawings related to the war on the home front? We see many posters of the war in drug store windows, why not see some artwork of what we're doing here at home? Your drawing sparked the idea, actually. Would you be interested?"

"Maybe."

"Well, we're asking for submissions that show how the war is affecting us here in the states. You know, a drawing of someone working in their victory garden, or maybe high school kids selling scrap metal to raise money for the war effort. Or maybe a picture of POWs working on a farm. The winner will get some new art supplies, and six free art lessons with a famous artist who lives here in Lancaster. I bet you'd have an excellent chance of winning."

John heard the kitchen screen door squeak open behind him.

"I might have some drawings that fit that idea," he said.

"Excellent. Then we'll hear from you again. Keep your eye on the paper. We'll publish the details soon."

"John?" Sarah walked up beside him. "You have a phone call." She looked at the reporter.

"This is Mark Burnes. He's a reporter." John turned back to Burnes. "I have to go."

John stepped into the kitchen.

"Would you be able to answer a few questions for me, young lady?" he heard before the door shut behind him. John looked back outside.

Sarah waved a hand at him. He didn't have time to go back out there and try to make her keep her mouth shut. But he did not like the idea of Sarah with the reporter.

John headed toward the office, where the Miller's had their phone. It took him so long to walk with his crutches, he hoped the person hadn't hung up.

"Hello?"

"John? How are you, hon? How's your leg?"

"I'm okay, Mom."

"I saw your drawing in the paper. I saved it for you. It was no surprise to me you were over there drawing, but I hope you get your work done."

"I drew that during lunch. It wasn't a problem."

"John, those POWs don't bother you, do they? You're not scared of them?"

"No, Mom. And only the newspaper and radio people call them POWs. We just call them PWs. Anyway, they're good workers. Only that one that was in the paper caused trouble. The rest are fine."

"All right, then." His mother hesitated.

"What is it? Why did you call?"

"It's Pop. He's been injured."

"Injured how?" John asked. "Is he all right?"

"Don't worry, the doctor said he's going to make it. They've sent him back to the United States and he's arrived at a hospital in Philadelphia. I'm soon leaving to go to the hospital myself. When he's well enough, they'll send him home. So in a way this is good news. We'll have him back with us again. I just wanted you to know. I called Ben, too."

"Did you talk to Pop?"

"No, not yet. All I know is they said he'll take some time to heal. I might need you at home to help care for him when I'm at work. So you'll be able to come home soon. I know you never wanted to go away."

John guessed it wouldn't sound right at this point to say he liked it on the Miller farm. That he looked forward to getting up in the mornings, even with the throbbing pain in his leg. That he'd made friends. That he was eating the best food he'd ever had.

"Okay mom," John said. "Be careful driving."

CHAPTER NINETEEN

"They caught Klein." John watched Hans's face as he shared his news the next day. They had just finished lunch and were sitting on the grass, sorting tomato seeds.

Hans grew still. He looked up at John. "When?"

"Yesterday. A reporter was here. He told me."

"I wonder what will happen to him. They'll probably send him to another camp."

"As long as I don't see him again." John said. "You didn't like him either, did you?"

"He was full of threats—always creating trouble. He attacked a friend of mine for reading a book on American law. And he doesn't like any of us speaking English. He sees it as a sign of betrayal."

"Didn't he get in trouble?"

Hans shook his head, but didn't elaborate.

"The guard told me he's a real Nazi," said John.

"He would be proud to hear you say so."

John got the feeling Hans didn't like talking about the war, but he wanted to know what Hans thought about it.

"Why did you join the army?"

"I had to. All men my age had to join."

"Sarah's brother, Sam, didn't want to fight, so he's working at a hospital somewhere."

"We had no choice like that."

"Would you have joined if you had a choice?"

Hans shrugged. "Maybe. I joined Hitler Youth when I was young. It seemed fun at first. It was like a club. We didn't know how full of hatred Hitler was. We didn't know he was preparing us for war. We were just kids. We felt lucky. Important. But then little things began to change. In school they replaced our old books. We were taught a new version of history. We were taught to hate people who weren't like us. Hitler was very smart. Many youth believed everything he had to say."

"When the war started, what did you think you were fighting for?"

"Land. After World War I, a great deal of our land was taken and given to other countries. German people could not accept that. We wanted it back. And it was a hard time for us. Many people were hungry and didn't have work. Hitler promised to make our lives better. He made people feel hopeful again, and proud to be German."

"Did you believe in him?"

"At the beginning. But my parents were suspicious of him. They never trusted him, and they were right. He had ideas for this war that most German people didn't know about. I hear things about what he's doing and I don't know what's true. I only know I fought to survive, to see my family again."

John picked a blade of grass and put it between his teeth. "I'll go fight when I'm old enough, if the war is still going on," he said. "My dad taught me how to shoot a rifle. I'm good."

Hans looked at him. "War is worse than you imagine. I hope you won't need to see it."

"What was the worst part? For you?"

Hans grew still. "Seeing the eyes of dead friends looking up at you—in reality and then in your dreams. And the fear." Hans slowly shook the seeds onto a tray and spread them out to dry.

John liked it that Hans always gave him direct answers. He was finding that sometimes it was easier to be honest with a passing stranger, even a German PW, than people you lived around.

"My dad's coming home. He's already in the states."

Hans glanced up. "That's good news."

"I guess so. I mean I'll be glad to see him, but he's injured. I don't know how badly. They say he's going to make it, but that doesn't tell me much."

"It tells you he's going to live. That's a lot."

"Yeah, but I wonder what he'll be like."

Hans slowly pulled his fingers through the seeds. "Maybe your father is wondering also what it will be like to come home. Maybe he wonders what you will be like."

John put a tomato seed in his mouth and bit down on it.

"You like to chew on things, don't you?" Hans asked.

John laughed. "I guess so. I'm always hungry. These don't taste that great, though."

John tried to spit a seed up in the air. "You can't spit these very far."

"Let's see," Hans said, and put several in his mouth. He sucked in his cheeks and blew them out. "Not bad," said John. He put a handful in his mouth and took a deep breath.

"Hi, John."

John jerked his head toward Sarah's voice, but there was no holding back. If anything, the surprise of hearing Sarah's voice right by his ear made him spit harder.

Several seeds landed on her face and bounced off. One stuck on the bridge of her nose. She waved her hands in front of her face like a swarm of bees were after her.

"Oh my word! John! What are you doing?"

"Sorry." But he couldn't keep a straight face. He started laughing and couldn't stop.

John couldn't remember ever having seen Sarah blush before. She picked a seed off of her nose, at the same time tilting her chin up and trying to act in control, the way she always liked to be.

John glanced over at Hans. Hans acted like he was busy working—really concentrating on those seeds in the tray. But John could see his sides shaking.

"And to think I came here to do something nice for you. You could at least act sorry."

"I am," John said. "Honest."

"If you were feeling any kind of remorse, you wouldn't be bent over sideways, laughing your head off. I'm not even going to ask you now."

"Ask me what?"

"Never mind." Sarah turned and began walking back toward the house.

"Ask me what?" John called after her.

"What kind of cake you wanted. You'll be lucky if I bake one now," she yelled over her shoulder.

"Does she bake you a lot of cakes?" Hans asked with a grin.

"I guess it's for my birthday tomorrow. If she makes anything now, I'm going to be afraid to taste it."

CHAPTER TWENTY

"Here we are," said Mrs. Miller, setting a basket of corn in front of John's chair. "I appreciate you helping me with this."

"You pay me to work, Mrs. Miller, and I feel like I sit around half the time now. I'll husk corn all morning if you want."

Mrs. Miller laughed. "I won't need you to do that."

She sat heavily on the cushioned chair next to John and quickly began peeling down the pointed green leaves from the tip of the corn. The ripping sound reminded him of when he tore his pants at school. Within seconds the cleaned ear was put in an empty box in front of them. John realized this was going to be like shelling peas next to Sarah—he would finish about one ear of corn to Mrs. Miller's five. He tried pulling off the silky hair that clung to the kernels at a faster pace.

John could hear Reuben call out something from the cannery, then laughter from the men. The cannery was up and running again this morning for the first time since the explosion. He wished he was out there, but he still couldn't do much on his leg.

"Now, John, you know we've enjoyed having you here," Mrs. Miller said.

John looked up at her. He felt his stomach drop. Were they going to ask him to leave because he wasn't strong enough to help them anymore?

"Your mother just called. She's bringing your father home this afternoon. What a gift on your birthday! Jake will drive you home after lunch. I told your mother you'd be welcome to come back anytime, but don't feel bad if you can't. We have the PWs to help out now."

John yanked the husks off his second ear of corn without speaking. He was glad his father was coming home, but to leave today, just like that, was so unexpected.

John could hear pans banging in the kitchen where Sarah and Dorothy were working. He remembered his first day here, when he was asked to watch the children. When the PWs began working on the farm, some of the other families stopped bringing their kids, and fewer women came to work. He never had to baby-sit again. John remembered how uncomfortable he was when he found Hans talking to Dorothy in the shed. Now she liked to sit next to Hans at lunchtime and it didn't bother anybody. Everyone ate together at the picnic tables.

John shifted his mind back to his father. "Maybe my dad isn't hurt too badly if he's coming home already."

"Can you imagine what that must feel like, to come home to your family after being away for so long, and for such an awful reason?" Mrs. Miller looked at John's face. "You'll have changed in his eyes. You'll be taller, and your face will look older to him." She smiled. Crinkles around her eyes spread into her round cheeks. "And now a fourteen-year-old young man."

Dorothy stepped out onto the porch. "We're making something special for you, John," she said with a wide grin. "But it's a surprise."

"Hush, Dorothy," Sarah said, following her outside.

"John, why don't you get packed up before lunch?" Mrs. Miller suggested. Don't forget your art materials on top of the cabinet in the kitchen."

"What do you mean, packed up?" Sarah asked, looking startled.

"John is going home this afternoon. His father is coming home."

"Oh." Sarah stared at John as he stood up and grabbed his crutches. "I'll help you pack, John," she said.

John wondered if she was eager for him to go. "That's all right. I don't have much stuff."

Sarah's eyes were still focused on his face, but John couldn't tell what she was thinking. He looked down and began walking.

"I can at least get your art things for you." She followed him into the kitchen. "Oh, and I wanted to show you the newspaper! They have that art contest advertised. You have to enter, John."

Sarah handed him a page cut from the newspaper. "Take it with you."

John tossed his clothes into the burlap bag he arrived with and glanced out the second-story window. The smell of cooking tomatoes drifted from the cannery through the open window. Tomatoes would always remind him of his time here.

John heard the dinging of the lunch bell and walked outside. He was going to eat a lot. He had no hopes that his mother had become a better cook since he'd been away, or that there was more food at home.

John sat across from Hans and Dorothy at the picnic table. Sarah sat down on his right and Fritz and Wilhelm—the newer PW with fading bruises on his face—sat on his left side. He wondered what his father would think if he drove up the lane and saw him now.

A large platter of corn on the cob sat in front of him. John reached for one after Reuben said a prayer. He noticed Fritz and Hans staring at him as he put butter and salt on it and raised it to his lips.

"What?" he asked Hans. "Why are you looking at me like that?"

"Corn is for pigs!" Hans said, genuinely looking perplexed.

John didn't know whether to laugh or be insulted.

"Just because pigs like corn doesn't mean I can't like it too," he said, biting into the sweet white kernels.

He glanced at Sarah. She shrugged.

"You don't eat corn?" she asked Hans.

"I've never seen people eat corn like this," he said. "Isn't it hard?"

Sarah laughed. "No," she said. "It's delicious. This is called sweet corn. We grow it to eat it. It's not the hard kind we give to pigs. That's called field corn."

"Don't you have corn where you come from?" Dorothy asked with wide eyes.

"I've never had this kind," said Hans. Hans imitated John, spreading butter over an ear of corn.

"I still wonder if this is some kind of joke to play on us," he said.

Sarah laughed again. She and John were the ones staring now, as Fritz and Hans hesitantly brought the ears of corn to their mouths.

"*Gut!*" said Fritz.

Hans nodded, and took another bite of corn, juice squirting from the kernels.

John ate quickly and opened his sketchpad, which he had brought outside with him. He looked at Hans and began to draw.

"This is messy eating," Hans said. "I don't think you want to draw this."

John grinned. "Yes, I do," he said. "So don't eat too fast."

"You need to hold the ear a little higher, Hans," said Jake, who had joined them. "Move your elbows out to the side more. Like this." Jake stuck his elbows almost straight out as he took a bite.

Hans began to imitate him until Fritz burst out laughing.

"Don't listen to him," Dorothy said. "He's just being dumb."

"Thank you, Dorothy," Hans said. "And now that I know the correct way to eat it, I think I'll try again with another . . . ear. Why do you call the corn an ear?"

"I don't know," said Dorothy. "It doesn't look like an ear."

"I read," said Sarah, "that the original meaning of the word ear, as in ear of corn, is spike or point. The word ear, as in ears attached to our head, came from a different word. Spelled Y-E-R-E, or something like that. So an ear of corn isn't supposed to look like an ear on your head. It means it looks pointy."

Fritz elbowed Hans, as if he wanted an interpretation.

Hans began to speak in German, then stopped and shrugged his shoulders.

"You have too much time on your hands," Jake said to Sarah, shaking his head, "if you know things like that."

"If you ever feel like reading, I have the book where I read that up in my room," Sarah said. "I'll loan it to you anytime."

Jake snorted, picked up his plate, and walked away.

"Can I borrow it?" John asked. "I ran out of stuff to read, and I have to sit around half the time." He put some finishing touches on his drawing, signed his name at the bottom, and pushed it over to Hans.

"For you," he said. "To remember your first time eating corn on the cob."

Hans smiled. "Thank you. I will like having this."

"I'm leaving today, so I wanted to give you something."

"Leaving? Why?"

"My father is coming home. I can hardly believe it. I'm going this afternoon."

"You must be excited," said Sarah.

John nodded, but didn't reply. How he thought he should feel and how he was feeling were two different things. He was excited about seeing his dad again, but he was also nervous. His stomach was churning, and he couldn't shake the sense of sadness that had settled over him. He couldn't wait to hug his dog, and to see that his dad was okay, but he would miss the Miller farm—the hectic pace, mealtimes, the people, even the PWs.

"John is going to enter an art contest," Sarah said to Hans. "Sponsored by the newspaper."

"That's good. What is the prize?"

"Free drawing lessons, and art supplies," Sarah said excitedly. "John certainly has a good chance of winning, don't you think?"

"I don't know who he would be competing against," said Hans. "But he has wonderful talent. He draws older than his age."

"I think you mean beyond his years," said Sarah. "That's what we would say."

"I will keep my eye on the newspaper. To see if you win," Hans said.

"I haven't decided to do it yet."

Sarah poked her finger into his side. "That's ridiculous."

"Stop poking me, I'm thinking about it."

Jake came back carrying the truck keys. "You ready, John?"

"You can't go yet!" Sarah said, jumping up from the bench. "Wait here, John."

Sarah ran toward the house, with Dorothy on her heels.

Sarah returned with a golden cake with strawberries nestled in the center. Dorothy stuck four candles along an edge.

"We don't have enough candles, John," Dorothy said. "You'll have to pretend there are fourteen. And we couldn't make icing because we didn't have enough sugar. We put some honey in the cake, though."

"It's perfect, Dorothy. It looks amazing." John had never had a birthday cake that looked as good as this one did. He smiled at Sarah.

Sarah smiled back, then struck a match and lit the candles. "Start us off, Reuben," she said.

Reuben stepped forward, his strong tenor voice filling the air with "Happy Birthday."

Mrs. Miller and Kenny each carried out a wooden ice-cream churn, setting them in the grass near the picnic tables.

"Who wants the first turn, while it's easy?" asked Mrs. Miller.

Kenny and Dorothy each claimed a handle, turning it in circles as the ice crunched with the movement.

Mr. Miller appeared with a banjo and began to pluck the strings. Reuben pulled a harmonica from his pocket and played the melody of a song John didn't recognize, the rich hum energizing the noon summer air.

John grinned. He didn't know Mr. Miller could play the banjo or Reuben a harmonica. John watched Mr. Miller's fingers pluck the strings faster and faster.

Fritz stood up and began to dance. He danced with his eyes closed—his long legs kicking and turning in perfect time to the music. Hans began to clap, and the other PWs joined in.

John knew the Millers' religion preached against dancing, but they didn't seem to mind Fritz enjoying himself. John bit into the slice of golden cake before him. This was a birthday he'd remember. Friends, food, music, and Fritz, with his eyes open now, laughing, spinning, enjoying life for what it was at this moment.

CHAPTER TWENTY-ONE

The house was silent except for the steady ticking of the grandfather clock and the occasional soft, sighing sound of Pepper's breathing. The quiet rhythms made him feel at home, but John also had an uneasy sense of things being different—like he was no longer the same person he had been the last time he'd stood in this kitchen. He sat down at the table to look through the mail. Pepper rested his head on John's knee. He'd followed John everywhere from the second he got home. "Have you been lonely, boy?" he asked, rubbing the dog's side. "Don't worry, I didn't abandon you."

John leafed through the new issue of *Life* magazine. Paintings and drawings of war scenes were featured, just like his dad had mentioned. John didn't know what provoked him more—bright red blood pouring from a soldier's head, or the shell-shocked eyes of a young man who leaned into the arms of another soldier. John thought the paintings showed the war in ways black-and-white photographs couldn't capture—colorful and beautiful and horrible. They made you proud of the soldiers, but also made you want to cry. He wondered what would happen to all these paintings after the war was over.

He pulled out some of the sketches he'd drawn on the Miller farm. He had to enter that art contest. And win. Not only did he desperately need new art supplies, but the announcement in the paper said Robert Watson would be giving the lessons. John had seen some of his work in a library book. The idea of working with him made John's heart race.

John laid out his drawings. There was Klein by the cornfield, Hans and Fritz eating lunch on the day they arrived at the farm, Sarah working in the garden, some PWs picking tomatoes in the greenhouse. Glancing through the drawings, he could almost feel the energy of the farm.

He loved the one of Hans writing in the Bible on the porch. Dorothy was watching intently by his side, standing very close, and it looked as if her chin was pointing to the PW letters on Hans's left shirtsleeve. Hans's forehead was wrinkled in concentration, his eyes calm and focused. A closed Bible sat to the side of the table. John liked the strangeness of it, of watching a PW writing in a Bible. Hans had said he learned calligraphy at a POW camp. John didn't know why they would teach something like that to PWs. But here Hans was, using this new skill to carefully write an American child's name in a family Bible.

But what would the judges think? Would they like it? What would the neighbors think? Would they get angry that Hans wasn't doing hard, physical work? Would they find fault with the Millers for letting a German PW write in their Bibles? John ran his fingers through his sun-streaked hair. This was his best drawing. He knew it.

John picked up the drawing of Hans lying in the grass after the fire. He had used some colored chalk on this one. He wanted the red burn marks on Hans's arm to stand out. Hans had no shirt on, and black streaks ran across his body. There was a large, jagged scar on his right side, and some smaller ones across his arms and chest. He had a soldier's body, but at that moment he was a young man collapsed on the grass, shielding his eyes from the sun, after helping to save John from the fire. In the distance John had drawn flames coming from the cannery, and men fighting them, some in PW clothes, some in farmers clothes. He didn't think people would find fault with this drawing. But the theme of the contest was, "How the War Affects You at Home." The PWs were captured enemy soldiers, working on an American farm. Would that be enough of a connection? Would that be what the judges were looking for?

Maybe he should send the one he'd started of the PWs picking tomatoes. It wouldn't take him long to finish it. Sarah, Dorothy, Kenny, and Jake were picking tomatoes as well. If American men weren't away at war, the Millers wouldn't be picking tomatoes side by side with PWs. John thought the judges might like the positive, everyday feel of this drawing instead of the fire and Hans lying shirtless with his scars showing.

John was studying a drawing of Hans and Fritz when he heard the car. He quickly gathered his work and limped to his bedroom. He laid his sketchpad and some loose drawings carefully in a dresser drawer, under some pants. He didn't want his dad seeing these. Not yet.

He grabbed his crutches and hurried toward the front door. The car had already come to a stop when he stepped onto the porch. John saw his father sitting on the passenger side. That was a first. His mother drove like she cooked—a little absentmindedly. His dad usually refused to get into the car if she was behind the wheel. John grinned and waved. He couldn't believe Pop was home.

His mom opened the car door. Her face looked strained, but she smiled when she saw John.

"John, dear, how are you?" she called as she walked around to his dad's side of the car. "I won't know how to hug you with those things under your arms."

"I'm okay, mom." John maneuvered himself down the steps. "How's Pop?"

His mom didn't answer. She opened the passenger car door. "Just wait here while I get your chair."

"What else would I do?" his dad asked sharply.

John walked slowly toward the car.

"Tell the boy to go inside."

"Oh, Ted. He's your son. He's so eager to see you."

"He's not watching this."

"I'll need him to help get your chair up the steps."

John stood glued to his spot a few feet away from the car. He watched his mother open a wheelchair, lean toward his father, and wrap her arm around his back. His dad grabbed the car door and helped pull himself up and into the wheelchair. For a second John thought he wouldn't make it. As he was beginning to sit, the chair started to move. His mother stuck her foot out to stop it and somehow found the strength to help lift his dad into the chair at the same time.

John sucked in his breath. His dad had no legs. They were cut off right above the knees, the stumps wrapped in white bandages.

John quickly jerked his gaze away from the damaged legs and looked up into his father's eyes.

"John."

"Hi, Pop."

"You've grown."

"Yeah." John wanted to hug his dad. But something in his dad's eyes warned him to stay where he was.

"What happened to you?" his dad asked.

John couldn't think straight. "What? Oh." He looked down at his leg. "I got burned a little in a fire. Not here. At the farm."

"Come greet your father properly, John," his mother said, as she spread a thin blanket over his dad's lap.

"It's good to have you home, Pop." John awkwardly put his arm around his dad's shoulder and hugged him. His dad didn't hug him back, but he gripped John's arm and squeezed.

"You've gotten some meat on these arms," his dad said.

"I hope you didn't eat more than your share at the Miller's." His mother hugged him tightly.

"No, Mom. I don't think so."

"Well, all the better you have some muscles now. I need you to help me get your father's chair up on the porch."

John glanced at his dad, who sat with two fists clenched in his lap.

"Where's Ben?" his dad asked.

His mother began to push the chair. "He'll be here in a couple of hours. They have so much work on the farm, I told him to come at dinnertime. John, if you can grab the chair from the bottom and lift a bit. . . . there, just like that."

John had laid one crutch down so he had a free hand. The wheelchair rubbed against John's burned leg as he helped lift and guide it up the three stairs. It hurt so much, all he could do was stand still for a minute, taking the weight off, and wait for the pain to ease. But at least he could still feel, and walk. He wouldn't complain.

His dad pushed his way into the house, turning the wheels of the chair with his arms.

"Ben asked if he could keep working on the farm," his mom said as she trailed behind. "I didn't know what to say. We do need the money, but I wasn't sure how soon you'd need him in the shop . . ."

"He should stay at the farm," his dad interrupted. "He was always a good worker. Someone has to earn money around here."

"Don't worry about money, Ted. I'll keep my job at the factory. John can help around here, since it doesn't look like he can work anywhere else right now."

"I can help you here," John said, "or go back to the Miller farm. There are things I can do there. I was still earning money."

"What can you do with that leg?" his dad asked, impatient fury escaping with his clipped words.

"I sorted tomato seeds, helped with garden stuff. They told me to come back if I wanted more work."

"Sounds like they were doing you a favor. You didn't sit around and draw before you did your work, did you?"

"No, sir." John hadn't, but he felt his face getting red anyway. "I never got a chance to thank you for the drawing you sent to me. It was terrific getting that in the mail. I couldn't believe it."

"It was Al's idea. We thought we were finished when our ship was bombed, minutes after he handed me that picture. But we both made it. Another ship was close by and picked us up. I even managed to save the drawing." His dad wheeled himself toward the kitchen window. "Then Al got shot—about a week before a landmine ripped me apart. I don't even know how he's doing—if he's alive or dead."

John's dad spoke quietly, almost as if he was talking to himself as he stared out the window. He turned his chair around abruptly.

"You can keep the drawing, but I don't want to see it lying around." He wheeled his chair toward the kitchen table, picked up a *Life* magazine, and leafed through it. He stared at the drawing of the soldier on the stretcher. "I don't want to see these, either," he said, and tossed the magazine on a chair.

CHAPTER TWENTY-TWO

"Well, you'll surely want to see a drawing John did. It made him a bit of a hero around here," his mother said.

"Mom, not now," John said. "Pop, are you hungry? Mrs. Miller sent tomatoes and fresh corn over. Even some chicken casserole."

His dad shook his head. "What's your mother talking about?"

"Right here," she said, as she put a newspaper into his dad's hands. "John drew that man—an escaped POW. They caught him because of it."

His dad stared at the paper.

"And here," his mother continued. "Here's an article they wrote about John. 'John Witmer has an amazing talent for drawing people's faces,' Sarah Miller said. 'He . . .'"

"I can read it myself," his dad said, jerking the paper away from John's mother. He looked up at John. "I can't believe my son had to be around POWs."

John shrugged. "They just come to work. They pick tomatoes."

"I'm glad you helped catch him boy, but you're not going back to that farm to work. I don't want you around Nazis."

His dad rubbed his eyes. "I need to lie down."

John watched his dad wheel himself toward the bedroom. His mother followed, running her fingers up and down the sides of her skirt, as if any wrinkles had to be smoothed out before she reached the bedroom.

The trill of the phone made him tear his gaze away. He walked over to a table in the corner of the kitchen.

"Hello?"

"May I speak with John, please?"

"Sarah?"

"John! Your voice sounded different. How are you?"

"I'm alright. What's going on there?"

"The usual. Some people are picking tomatoes, some are in the cannery.

Listen, since my dad was away when you left, he said to make sure you know you're welcome to come back to the farm to work whenever it suits. There will be work for you, even with your sore leg. Just give us a call and someone will run over for you."

"I appreciate that, Sarah. Tell your dad I said so. And I'd like to come back and work, but I think I'll need to stay here and take care of my dad."

"How is he, John?"

John couldn't bring himself to tell Sarah his dad had lost his legs. He was still getting used to the truth of it himself. "Okay, I guess," he said. "He has to get used to being home again."

"Well, I hope he heals quickly. Where was he injured?"

"His legs."

"Oh my. You all have some bad legs over there. Is he on crutches too?"

"No."

"Well, that's good. Dorothy's here. She said to tell you she misses you."

John closed his eyes. It already seemed like a long time since he'd been at the farm.

"Tell her hi," John said. "Tell her to draw me some pictures of what people are doing there."

"I'll tell her. And don't forget to choose your drawings for the contest. I'm going to keep pestering you until you do."

"I'm working on it."

"Working on it how?"

"It's complicated, Sarah. I have to choose the right drawings. I don't want to offend anyone."

"There you go again with your worrying. You should have left them with me. I'd be able to choose for you. Just mail some. They're all good, so you can't go wrong."

"I don't have a large envelope. Or stamps." John felt like he was a small child making excuses. But it was the truth.

"So, after you decide which drawings to enter, call me and I'll send Jake to pick them up. I mean it, John. Jake drives near your home on his way to town almost every day. We have all kinds of envelopes here in the office. I'll send them for you."

"I'd pay you later. For everything."

"All right. But don't worry about that. I just don't want you to miss the deadline. You have until August 14."

"I know. Thanks, Sarah." John didn't tell her the new reason he had for not entering the contest—that it might make his father angry. There was nothing she could do to fix that.

"Well, I have to get back to work." Sarah hesitated. "I hope you can come back soon."

"Me, too. But it's good to be home," he added quickly.

CHAPTER TWENTY-THREE

"You can help me out in the shop this morning."

John glanced over at his dad. After two weeks of being holed up in the house, John wasn't sure what had triggered his dad's interest in going outside.

"Sure, Pop."

John swallowed his last bite of oatmeal. It was thick and sticky and half-cold. His mom had made it before leaving for work. John figured he had to learn how to cook. He had gotten used to Mrs. Miller's cooking and wasn't ready to sacrifice his taste buds without a fight.

"You ready?" his dad asked as he began to push himself to the front door. "I need to make a ramp for the porch so I can get in and out of this house by myself. Hopefully this is the last time you have to help me get down these steps."

John needed his arms to help his dad, so he left his crutches in the kitchen. New skin was forming where he had been burned, and it felt tender and stiff. He tried not to limp as he walked outside.

His dad waited by the steps. John grasped the handles of the wheelchair tightly and tilted the chair up. The steps were narrow, but they were the only way down. He began to slowly push the chair forward. But as soon as the back wheels started rolling down the steps John had to go fast. He couldn't have stopped that chair if he wanted to. Bump! Bump! Bump! The chair rattled as it landed on the concrete walkway.

"I'm lucky I have teeth left after that," his dad grumbled.

John pushed his dad to the shop and brushed off some of the spider webs from the door. He flipped the "Closed" sign to "Open." He knew they weren't really open for business, but it felt good to do that anyway.

His dad wheeled himself inside and ran his hands over the counter. "Feels strange to be in here," he said.

John walked around the small shop. A thick layer of dust covered the tables, the tools, the chairs. He wiped off the dust from a stool with his hand and sneezed.

"Let's see if we can get this place cleaned up," his dad said. "Why don't you get some rags and water from in the house? Stuff out here is too dirty to even clean with."

John went inside and brought back an armload of cleaning supplies. He opened the windows and propped open the door to try to draw some fresh air into the room, but there was no breeze and the musty smell of a closed up room wasn't going anywhere. It seemed to John the dust rose up as he wiped his cloth across the counter, and settled back down as soon as he moved on to a new area of the room.

His dad was slowly, meticulously cleaning his tools. With the wheelchair behind a table, John couldn't see his dad's lower body. John felt like he was actually seeing a glimpse of the father he remembered.

His dad's deep voice broke the silence. "How'd you burn your leg?"

"A fire started in the cannery, near the boiler."

"How'd that happen?"

John shrugged. "Don't know. There was some kind of explosion. Took everyone by surprise. I was climbing the steps to go up to the second floor when it happened, and I fell. My pant leg caught fire."

"How'd you get it out?"

"I don't remember much. I hit my head on the floor. Somebody told me one of the PWs put it out and got me away from the fire."

His dad made a grunting noise. "Was it the one who escaped? The one in the newspaper?"

"No. That one was mean. He wouldn't help anybody."

"So you just decided to draw a mean PW during your lunch break." John saw his dad slightly shake his head. "You and those drawings, boy. Never would have imagined one of them would catch a Nazi. At least you recognized trouble when you saw it."

"Pop, there's a contest being sponsored by the newspaper. A reporter told me they got the idea after printing my drawing in the paper. It's an art contest. They want pictures of how the war affects us here at home. If you win, you get free art supplies and drawing lessons. I thought I'd send in a couple of my drawings and give it a try."

John held his breath. He hadn't planned to tell his dad about the contest. But it seemed like he was in a good mood, and it'd be better if he knew about it. John wasn't ready to show him the pictures he'd drawn, though, especially not after his reaction to the drawings in *Life* magazine.

"Find me some boards for the ramp," his dad said. "Over there in that pile. Maybe some of that oak."

He didn't say a word about the contest, and John didn't press him. He guessed no comment was better than a negative one.

John pulled some large pieces of wood over to his dad, who had started the power saw. His dad measured one of the boards and held it up to the saw. John watched the saw neatly cut five inches off the board. He handed his dad the next board, and had started to turn away to grab another one when he noticed his dad's fingers. They were trembling. Just a little, but enough to make John wonder if he could hold onto the board the way he needed to. Then his dad's left arm jerked—too close to the saw, which would cut a man's finger off in a split second.

"Pop! Watch out!" John yelled, as he yanked the wheelchair backwards. The wood clattered to the floor. John stood behind his dad, his breath coming quickly. His dad sat as still as the board lying by his side. Suddenly the noise of the saw seemed too loud, too overpowering. John reached around his dad and turned it off.

"What happened?" John asked. "What's wrong with your arm?"

His dad shook his head, turned his wheelchair around, and pushed himself outside.

"Help me into the house, then come back out here and finish the ramp," his dad said. There was no more life in his voice. John had to strain to hear him.

"It'll probably get better, Pop. Maybe with some rest . . ."

"Enough, boy."

John managed to get his father into the house, and then returned to the shop to build the ramp. For once he was glad he had carpentry skills. It might not be what he wanted to do for the rest of his life, but at least it made him useful. John knew Ben could have built the ramp in half the time it took him, but he'd get the job done.

It felt like he was ripping open the new skin on his leg as he dragged the heavy wood to the porch after he had cut the boards to size. John kept working, needing to finish the job before he gave in to the pain. He pounded a final nail into the hard wood that formed a ramp from the back porch. The ramp didn't look bad, but he hoped the slant wasn't too steep.

"Pop?" he called out. "Want to come try this out?"

John went into the house.

"Pop? Where are you?" The house was quiet. Pepper stood outside the door of John's room. He nudged it with his nose. John could feel his heart speed up. Was his dad in there?

"Pop?" he called out, and pushed the door open. His dad's chair was parked next to the dresser, the middle drawer open. John's pants, which had covered his sketchbook, lay on the floor.

John's dad held a drawing in his shaking hands. His face was pale, his eyes narrowed, as he stared at the picture.

"I couldn't find my aspirin and thought you might have some," he said. His voice was quiet, but the whispered words had a sharp, steely, edge. "This is what I find instead." He looked up at John, his angry dark eyes now staring at John's face like he didn't know him.

John looked down at the drawing his dad held. It was the one of Hans writing in the Bible. John bit his lower lip. He had never planned to let his dad see that drawing. Ever.

His dad picked up another picture—the one of Hans and Fritz eating lunch.

"You like this man? He's in every picture."

His dad slowly ripped the drawing in half, straight through the face of Hans. John watched one piece fall to the floor.

"Well, I don't like any of them. You understand?"

"I just drew what I saw."

"You seem awfully fascinated by these PWs. And you didn't answer my question. You like this man?"

"He's okay. They're not all the same, Pop. He's the one that helped me . . ." John stopped and swallowed. He looked at Hans' nose, ripped in half, lying in front of his feet.

"They all seemed the same when they were shooting at me. I couldn't tell a bit a difference then."

His dad shook the torn paper he held in his hand. "Were these the drawings you wanted to enter in that contest?"

His dad pulled the sketchbook out of the drawer and shoved the loose drawings inside. "I'll burn these before they're entered in a contest."

"No, Pop!" John yelled. "I won't send them in!"

"Move aside, John."

John doubled his fists, rage roaring through his shaking body. He snatched the sketchbook from his dad's lap. His dad grabbed at his arm, but John dodged away.

"Give me those drawings!" his dad said slowly, as he inched his chair forward.

John swept up the torn image of Hans from the floor, and ran.

"Don't you leave this house! I'll come after you, boy, I swear I will!" were the last words John heard as he stumbled onto the porch.

CHAPTER TWENTY-FOUR

John was at the end of their short lane when he heard the door slam at the house. He didn't turn around. He couldn't believe he was running from his dad, but he also couldn't believe his dad wanted to burn his drawings. John knew his dad would be coming after him if he could, that he was going out of his mind with frustrated rage that he was stuck in a wheelchair and making empty threats.

John put the sketchbook in a basket on the back of his bike and quickly pushed off with his good leg. He flinched as he put pressure on his injured leg. The new red, blotchy skin almost looked the same as when he'd fallen off his bike a couple of years ago and gotten a bad case of road rash. It felt worse, though, and John knew this would be the longest four-mile bike ride of his life.

He'd head to the Miller farm. But what would he tell them? Sarah and Mrs. Miller would fuss at him for abusing his leg. Would they believe he'd put himself through this just to visit?

After a couple of miles he reached the old covered bridge and entered into its semi-darkness. The tires of his bike bumped over the wooden boards. It was too much. He slid from the seat and walked the bike through the bridge. Beneath it, the stream was running low but was still moving over the rocks. He walked to the edge of the bank and cupped his hands together to get a drink, then dipped his forehead down into the icy cold water. He felt sick all over. He wished he could lay down in the grass and forget about everything—with the water gurgling nearby, and the peace of the hazy, hot afternoon filtering through the thick-leafed trees—but inside he was so worked up he felt like an angry bull running wild.

He rested a few minutes before slowly climbing back on his bike. He wanted to get this ride over with. He began to peddle, trying to build up some speed before he hit the hill around the next curve. The pain was so intense that tears blurred his vision. So what if he cried now? It felt good to not fight it. He'd pull himself together before he got there.

The PWs were finishing lunch when John finally rode down the Miller's lane. Reuben held up his hand in a wave. John let his bike drop and slowly limped toward the picnic tables, carrying his sketchbook. He had to sit soon, or he felt he would fall over.

"John! What are you doing here?" Reuben called to him.

"Just came for a visit," John said, trying to sound cheerful.

Fritz came out of the outhouse. He said something in German, scrunched up his nose, and waved his hand in front of his face. The men began to laugh.

"He was in there a long time for not liking the smell," said Jake.

Reuben must have translated this, because the men laughed harder.

"We're heading back to the greenhouses, John," Reuben said. "Go to the kitchen to get some food if you haven't eaten. At least get a drink of water. You look pale."

Hans stopped at John's side as the men began to leave. "Already riding a bike?"

John nodded. Hans would know better than anyone that his leg was far from ready to ride a bike. The constant stretching and strain of the skin on his ankle when peddling made no sense for someone trying to heal a burn wound. Hans wasn't wearing a bandage on his arm today, and it still looked red and sore.

"John Witmer! What are you doing here?" Sarah called out as she came out of the kitchen, the screen door banging behind her.

"She's a pretty girl," Hans said with a smile. "Maybe she's the reason you worked hard to get here."

"I came," John said, "because my dad . . ." John shook his head. Should he tell Hans about his problems with his father?

"Maybe you can talk to your friend about it," Hans said.

"She won't understand." John looked at Hans, all of a sudden feeling desperate to hear his opinion. "My dad's so angry and bent up inside," he blurted out. "He's in a wheelchair. He lost his legs."

Hans looked at John for a few seconds. "You can't make the anger go away. He has to work it out himself. It has nothing to do with you."

"But I make it worse. He hates my drawings, and he found them. He started tearing them up."

Sarah reached the picnic table where John was sitting. Strands of curly hair escaped from her loose bun as usual, framing her tanned face. She bent down and looked at John, her eyebrows drawn together. "You look terrible," she said.

"Thanks."

"I must go," said Hans, looking over at Pete, who was signaling the men to get moving. "Are you staying here for a while, John?"

"I just came to visit for a little bit," said John. "I can't stay long."

"Maybe we'll see you another day, then," said Hans. He nodded at the sketchbook. "You have all your drawings with you?"

"Yeah."

"That's good," Hans said, and then took off after the other men.

Sarah sat down at the picnic table. "What did he mean by that?" she asked. "And how did you get here?"

"Bike."

Sarah shook her head. "That was a foolish thing to do. Look at you. You aren't fit to ride a bike."

"I made it."

Sarah glanced down at John's sketchbook. "I told you Jake would come to pick up your pictures," she said. "Why on earth did you bring them yourself?"

"I wanted to."

Sarah eyes narrowed in annoyance. "Well, you're in a mood, aren't you?"

John didn't answer. He guessed he was.

"Have you eaten?" Sarah asked.

"No."

"Come on to the kitchen then," she said.

"Can I just wait here?" John couldn't stand the thought of moving his leg again.

"Fine," Sarah said. "But you're sure acting peculiar."

Sarah returned with a large bowl of bean soup and some homemade applesauce. John thought the awful bike ride might have been worthwhile just for that first taste of Mrs. Miller's soup.

"Have you decided which drawings you're going to enter in the contest?" Sarah asked. She was sitting across from him, her green eyes watching him intently.

"I'm having a hard time with that."

"Well, let me see," Sarah said, reaching for the sketchbook.

John didn't feel like arguing with her. He didn't know how to explain that entering the contest was complicated, maybe impossible.

"I think the one with Hans writing in the Bible is your best one," she said.

"That doesn't really have to do with how the war is affecting us at home," John said. "And it would make people angry, anyway."

"Why should someone writing a name in a Bible make people angry? He was doing us a favor."

John shook his head. "I'm not sending that one in."

Sarah continued to flip through the drawings. Her fingers stilled as she stared at one in particular.

"John," she whispered.

John looked up, startled at her tone of voice.

"Is this your dad?" she asked.

John had forgotten he had that one in there—a drawing of his dad in his wheelchair, out on the porch. He had thought his dad looked heroic in his uniform. The look on his face was hard to read. Some sadness, some anger, and maybe some relief at being home. John drew it the day his dad returned. He had sat inside to sketch, looking at his dad from the window. His dad surely would have ripped this one up had he seen it.

"He's in a wheelchair? Why didn't you tell me? What happened?"

John shrugged. "A landmine. He doesn't say much about it."

Sarah stared at John, her eyes wide. "Is he in pain?"

"Probably. But sometimes I think he has more pain inside his head than he does in his body."

Sarah bit her lower lip. "I don't know how your dad would feel about the idea, but this picture, John—it would win. There's something about his eyes—like he's impatient, calm, and alert all at the same time."

"My dad found my drawings, Sarah. The ones of the PWs. He was so mad, he ripped one up. He went crazy at the idea of sending them in to the contest."

"Oh, John," Sarah said, covering his hand with hers. "That's too bad. What did you do?"

"I grabbed my sketchbook and came here." John looked down at Sarah's hand resting on top of his own. She had long fingers.

"I'm going to rest a bit, but then I need to go home again. I left my dad alone." John hoped his dad hadn't had any accidents. He had images of him falling out of his chair.

"Jake can drive you home," Sarah said. "And I'll go along. Maybe if I go in and say hi to him, maybe bring a loaf of bread or something, it will be easier for you."

"Nothing's going to make it easier, Sarah."

"Well, leave the drawings with me. If you decide to send them in, just call me. I'll get an envelope ready and everything. Maybe your dad would be proud of you if you won. Maybe it would change his mind."

John gave a disbelieving laugh, finding Sarah's idea ridiculous. But he had planned to leave them here anyway.

"Who's that?" Sarah asked, squinting at a car speeding down the lane, sending dirt and pebbles airborne in noisy bursts.

John watched the car and felt his stomach turn. It couldn't be.

"They need to slow down," Sarah said. "They should know there are usually little children running around a farm."

"Sarah, take my sketchbook inside. Hurry up." John shoved the drawings toward Sarah.

"Go! Don't come out again for a while either. Hide if you have to."

"What on earth John Witmer? Are you losing your mind?"

"That's my dad, Sarah!"

"Oh," Sarah said, getting up from the bench. "But what are you going to do? I know your dad's in a wheelchair, but will he . . ."

"Go, Sarah! I'll be fine. Please go."

John slid his legs out from under the picnic table. He slowly stood and began to walk toward the car, which pulled to a stop in the circular lane between the house and the greenhouses.

John saw Ben get out of the driver's side. His dad sat in the car, his fingers restlessly tapping the passenger door through the open window.

Reuben came out of a greenhouse to pick up an empty crate.

"Can I help you?" he heard Reuben call out.

"No, we're just here for John!" Ben yelled back.

John kept walking. He was dizzy. The sun was beating down, so bright, so hot, so stifling. He wanted morphine for his leg and a bed—the bed upstairs with the window he loved to look out of, especially in the evenings when the farm grew quiet. Instead he had to face his father, who was now watching him.

"Can't you move any faster?" Ben asked.

John didn't answer. He concentrated on putting one foot in front of the other. He couldn't believe it when he saw Hans come out of the nearest greenhouse. Stay there, Hans, he thought. Please don't walk over here.

His dad made a beckoning motion to John with his finger.

"We're going home," he said loudly, as John limped a few steps closer to the car. "Where are your drawings? Get them and get in here."

Hans stopped in his tracks.

John felt like he had nothing left. Nothing. He couldn't think.

He glanced toward the house, and there was Sarah, standing at his old window on the second floor. He thought it might be the first time she'd ever listened to him.

"What are you smiling at?" His dad sounded enraged, speaking through clenched teeth.

John jerked his head away from the window.

"I'm not getting my drawings, but I'll get in the car."

"John, can you just cooperate?" Ben said. "This is embarrassing now, but it could get out of hand. I've never seen Pop like this," he muttered so only John could hear.

Hans began to move again, coming closer to the car, a crate of tomatoes in his hands.

No, no, no, John thought, as he saw his dad's head turn toward the sound and then become still. The fingers stopped tapping.

"I figured I'd see some of his kind," he said. "He speak English?"

"Yes," John mumbled.

Hans continued walking.

"Don't come any closer," his dad said. "I got a rifle in the back seat."

Hans stopped and set down the crate of tomatoes.

"You're the one in John's drawings."

John moved toward the back door of the car, on the opposite side of his dad, his heart pounding. No way was Pop getting his rifle.

"Why does my son draw you so much? What are you using him for?"

"He draws everyone. He's very skilled."

"You stay away from him, you understand me?"

"Mr. Witmer! It's so nice to see you. I brought you some ice water. Thought you might be getting thirsty out here." Sarah seemed to appear out of nowhere, her blue pitcher in hand.

His dad stared at Sarah, visibly working at shifting his train of thought.

She held out a glass and he finally reached for the water. "Thank you," he said.

"Mother's asking if your family would like to come for supper tonight."

"Tell your mother thank you, but that's not necessary," John's dad said. He gave a small smile. "Though John let us know your mother is quite a cook."

Hans caught John's eye. "Reuben sent me out here with the tomatoes for your family. He said take however many you want."

"Thank you," John said. He could think of nothing else to say in this bizarre situation.

Hans began walking back to the greenhouse.

"Where's your guard? Why isn't anyone watching him?" John's dad asked Sarah.

"We have a guard. He's in the greenhouse with the other men. But we trust Hans."

John's dad shook his head.

"He saved John, you know. From the fire."

John inched toward the front of the car and stood near Sarah.

"This is what I know," his dad said. "He's the enemy. Nothing erases that."

Sarah stepped forward to take the empty glass John's dad held in his pale fingers.

"Well," she said after several moments. "You all want some tomatoes?" She looked at Ben. "Why don't you put some in the car? Take a lot if you can use them."

John licked his parched lips. He stood as still as he could, trying to keep any weight off his bad leg. He watched Ben gather tomatoes into his arms and took a step toward the car to open the door for him. But his leg was like rubber now, his eyes lost their focus, and it seemed like the car stretched away from his reach. He fell down to the pebbled driveway on his knees.

His embarrassment was as palpable as the sun beating down on his back.

"Your mother's a nurse, I hear," he heard his dad say. "Maybe she could have a look at him—if she has the time."

"Of course," Sarah said. She bent down and grasped John's arm.

"Can you stand with some help?" she whispered.

Ben walked over and draped John's other arm over his shoulder.

"C'mon," he said.

CHAPTER TWENTY-FIVE

John leaned out of his open window as Jake pulled the truck to a stop. At least Pop wasn't outside waiting for him. After the scene with his dad and Ben, he had ended up staying at the Millers. Mrs. Miller had insisted on keeping an eye on him for a couple of days. Now he had to deal with whatever awaited him at home.

"You sure you don't want me to come in?" Sarah asked again, digging her elbow into John's side.

"No, Sarah. Another time, thanks." Sarah sat between John and Jake in the truck.

"Well, take this then," Sarah said, placing a loaf of soft homemade bread on his lap.

"Thanks. And thanks for the ride," John said, as he climbed out. "See you."

"Yep," Jake said.

John's eyes met Sarah's and for a second he saw pity there. He didn't like that look coming from Sarah. He pulled his bike from the back of the truck and walked toward the house.

Ben was in the kitchen opening and closing cabinet doors.

"You looking for something to eat?" John asked. "Mrs. Miller baked this bread this morning. Here."

Ben turned around to look at John. "Thanks. You all right?" he asked.

"Yeah. Where's Pop?"

"Resting. Mom's at work." Ben sighed. "Wanna tell me what's going on before he wakes up? He won't tell me a thing except he wants to get his hands on some drawings of yours. That was the strangest afternoon I ever experienced when we drove out to that farm. I came home to Pop slamming around the house saying we had to go find you. I couldn't believe you had left him alone. You were supposed to be watching him."

"I know. I shouldn't have left. But he ripped up my drawing."

"Why? What in the world did you draw?"

"Some PWs. I wanted to enter a couple of the drawings in an art contest. Pop was against it."

"No kidding," Ben said, shaking his head.

John sank down onto a kitchen chair, welcoming Pepper as he placed his head on John's lap. John pulled a burr from the dark fur on Pepper's neck.

"So what's it like, working with PWs?" Ben asked.

"They're just men. Some mean and creepy, like that one who ran off. Some quiet, but nice enough. The ones at the Miller farm are good workers. The same men always come. We just, you know, pick tomatoes and stuff. They all want the war to end, same as we do. I drew them doing different things on the farm, and mixing with the Miller family. That's what got Pop so mad."

"John, I swear. Sometimes you don't think."

"That's been my day-to-day life and I draw what I see. I also drew Pop in his wheelchair, in his uniform, the day he came home. Sarah says it would win the contest."

"You can't send that in, John." Ben's voice had an edge to it now. "Pop would hate everyone staring at him in a wheelchair."

"I won't, but I didn't draw that picture to make Pop look bad or hurt him in any way. I was proud of him when I drew it. He looks a little sad, but he looks good too. I drew him as a soldier, wearing his uniform, back from fighting in the war."

"Can I see it?"

"Right now it's at the Miller's. I left them all there."

Ben smiled. "You know, if you drew things like flowers and trees, he wouldn't care."

"He'd care. He thinks drawing is a waste of time, especially for boys. But I was born with this itch in my fingers, Ben. It's something I can do well—about the only thing."

"It's the only thing you care about doing well, John. The only thing you try hard at. I think that's the main problem Pop has always had with you."

"Yeah? Well now I've decided to work hard at learning how to cook. That'll probably make him madder, since I'm sure he thinks that's women's work too. But at least he'll have something hot to eat when he wakes up."

CHAPTER TWENTY-SIX

John was placing several ears of corn in a pot of boiling water for supper when his dad came out of the bedroom. John turned around and looked at him. He wanted to face him head-on and get it over with.

Piercing dark brown eyes bore into him for several endless seconds. John sensed his dad yearned to strike him. John had felt the weight of his hand before. Not often, but a kid doesn't forget what that feels like. But John could see his dad's right hand shaking with tremors, and John had grown several inches since his dad had been away. Power had shifted, and they both knew it.

"Where's Ben?" his dad asked.

"Working in the garden."

His dad sat by the back window and stared out toward the garden. "Wasn't sure if your running away was temporary or for good," he said.

John felt his cheeks flush. "I was too mad to think about what I was doing."

The wheelchair creaked as it inched closer toward John. John resisted the impulse to step backward.

"You better start thinking. You ever defy me like that again, you won't stay living in this house. You understand me?"

"Yes, sir."

"I thought for sure I'd find you in a ditch somewhere. You could barely get out of the lane with that leg."

"I'm sorry I left you alone."

His dad quickly reached out and smacked a fly with the back of his hand. "I can be left alone now and then. God knows I crave it sometimes."

He stared at John for several seconds. "I changed my mind about your drawings. Don't bring them back. I don't want them in this house. They make me act in a way I'm not proud of. Too mad to think about what I'm doing. Isn't that how you put it?"

John nodded. He was shocked. His dad wasn't given to apologies, but this almost sounded like one.

"You have no idea what's it's like to spend a year of your life at war in another country, fighting, trying to survive, watching your friends die, only to turn around and see your enemy standing on your neighbor's lawn. And people are expecting you to have a polite little talk. Act like that's normal. I can't do that. Not now."

His dad wheeled his chair back to the window and pulled the curtain aside. He snapped his fingers and Pepper trotted over. His dad's hand reached out to stroke Pepper's thick fur.

"I can't make small talk," he said, his voice almost dropping to a whisper. "With anyone. Especially not with some young kraut who thinks he knows something about my son I don't know. 'He's very skilled,' he says, like he's telling me something new—like I want his opinion."

"Mom's here," Ben said, banging open the kitchen door. "And I'm starving, so let's eat."

John turned to slice the homemade bread Sarah had given him. His dad had made some good points, but John didn't know what to say in response. "I think you would like Hans if you got to know him," was what he wanted to say, but he knew his dad wasn't ready to hear anything like that. The bread was crumbling under his fingers until he learned the slices had to be thicker and he had to make a sawing motion with the serrated knife.

"John, isn't this lovely! Thank you for getting supper ready," his mom said, as she squeezed his arm.

John smiled into his mother's friendly eyes. "It's no problem, mom. You okay?" he asked, as she pressed a hand to her lower back.

"Oh yes. Bending over a sewing machine all day is hard on my bones, is all."

It felt strange to sit with his family at the table. It was the first meal they'd shared since his dad had gone to war. His mom did most of the talking, that hadn't changed.

"John!" she said abruptly. "I have something to show you!" His mother got up from the table and dug a piece of newspaper out of her bag.

"Can't it wait?" his dad asked.

"No, no. This is exciting, and I keep forgetting to give it to him. Here, John."

John read the newspaper ad, and looked up at his mother. She waited for his response, her eyes wide with expectation and pleasure.

"I know about it, mom. But thanks. I appreciate you saving it for me."

"What is it?" Ben asked.

"An art contest," his mom replied. "Perfect for your brother. They want drawings of how we're affected by the war here at home. You must have something, John. You could win free art lessons!"

The room grew quiet. Ben, who usually slapped butter on his bread and ate it in two bites, became very interested in spreading butter slowly and evenly.

John glanced at his dad, who finished cutting a tomato, then looked up, latching on to John's gaze.

"John Witmer. I thought you'd be excited," his mom said. "If you don't have anything ready, you can get busy drawing. You only have a few days left to enter."

John felt like there was a balloon hovering over the table, slowly expanding. With every word from his mother it stretched thinner—closer to bursting. Could his mother not feel the tension?

"Do you have any ideas?" his mother asked. "For the contest?"

"I don't want him entering," his dad said sharply. "John and I already discussed it."

"Oh, but people will be looking for his work," his mother said, reaching over to John and brushing the hair out of his eyes. "They'll be so disappointed if he doesn't enter. He's already famous you know, having his drawing of that PW in the paper. The paper might even call here if he doesn't send anything in. They'll think that it got lost or something."

"Would you pass the butter, please, Ben?" she asked. "Mmm, this corn is so good, isn't it? So what ideas do you have, John? Maybe a drawing of our victory garden? The sunflowers set off the vegetables so beautifully right now."

John had always thought his mother was a little slow to get things. And she'd ramble on about details that didn't matter in a tiring way, especially when there was a problem or disagreement to be dealt with. But now he wondered if she was actually clever—if she knew how to handle Pop in ways that hadn't been obvious to him before.

"I don't know, Mom. I think everyone will send in drawings of victory gardens. And ours is pretty small."

"Well, then, do you have anything else in mind? I'm sure you can come up with some wonderful ideas."

"He's fourteen years old. He has other things to do than draw pictures of sunflowers," his dad said, his deep voice slow and pleasant, yet challenging as he raised his eyebrows at John.

"He has a sore leg. He has to sit some of the time anyway. And John's so fast at drawing. It wouldn't take him long to whip something up. I've always been amazed at how fast he draws."

His dad shook his head.

"I've been talking about the contest with the ladies at the factory. They were all so impressed with his drawing of the PW. And the man being caught made it all the more impressive. Wilma thinks John will win for sure. They ask me every day if I've remembered to tell him about the contest. Tomorrow I can finally say yes, thank goodness. Then they'll begin asking me what he's drawing, I'm sure that'll be their next question, and . . ."

"Eleanor."

John watched his parents watch each other. His mother's shoulders dropped; veiled innocence left her eyes.

"He can send in the drawing he has of that Miller girl in the garden," his dad said.

John couldn't believe his ears.

"But that's it. That's the only one, you hear?"

John nodded once. He had just gotten permission to enter the contest, and he was glad. But he couldn't help feeling cheated out of being able to enter his best work. His drawings of the PWs would have made a different kind of impression on the judges. Everyone was curious about PWs; they couldn't help themselves.

"Where is this drawing, dear? May I see it?" his mom asked.

"It's at the Miller farm."

"Oh, well, let's drive there tomorrow morning and pick it up. I'll take it to the newspaper office on my way to work. It's not far from the factory."

John knew that wasn't really true. The factory wasn't in the city, where the newspaper office was. But he didn't question her, and neither did his dad.

"Okay, Mom," John said. They'd drive over to the Millers and get that one drawing. Maybe if his mom saw some of the other drawings, she'd like them too. Maybe she'd decide to risk defying his dad and take a couple more.

CHAPTER TWENTY-SEVEN

"What do you mean, they're not here?" John asked Sarah. "Keep looking!"

Sarah rummaged through the papers and envelopes on the desk in the office. "I've been looking, John. When you called to say you were coming, I came in here to get them. I've looked everywhere I can think of. I'm sorry, but the envelope is gone."

"How many drawings were in there?"

"Four, 'cause I wasn't sure which ones you'd want. There was the one of me in the garden, the PWs picking tomatoes in the greenhouse, Hans and the fire, and the one of Klein by the cornfields."

"What? I never even told the sheriff I had that one of Klein! I couldn't have entered that one."

"Well, the sheriff didn't need that one. But I thought the judges might go for it. A PW that actually did try to escape, standing by the edge of a cornfield. I thought you wouldn't care if that one was entered. You kept saying no to the other drawings I suggested."

"Where are the rest of my drawings?"

"In my room. Don't worry, they're safe."

John walked around the office. He bent and looked under the desk.

"I checked there."

John stood. He slammed his fist down on the desk. "How could you just lose them, Sarah? I trusted you with them!"

Sarah crossed her arms. "I said I was sorry."

"Do you think they were thrown away?"

"I can't imagine why they would have been. I had written the address of the newspaper on the envelope, and had it ready to mail. I was just waiting for your call. I wonder if it was . . ."

John looked up to see Jake standing in the doorway, with Hans behind him.

Jake walked into the office. "Come on in, Hans," he said.

John couldn't imagine why Hans was being invited into the office.

Hans smiled when he saw John and Sarah. "How's the leg?" he asked John.

"Better every day," John answered. "How about you?"

"Good. Thank you."

"What are you two doing in here?" Jake asked. "You need to clear out. Hans needs to use the desk."

Sarah stepped forward. "We're looking for a large yellow envelope with the address of the newspaper on it, for that art contest. Have you seen it?"

"Can't remember. But I mailed a stack of stuff this morning. Here Hans, sit at the desk. I'll get the pen and ink. The Bibles are over there. Mrs. Beiler brought over three. Hope you don't mind doing this again. Word seems to have spread."

"No," Hans said, taking a seat. "I am glad to do it."

John wondered when the neighbors had started bringing over their Bibles for Hans to write in. If Hans was working in the office, he could have taken John's drawings, or gotten rid of them. But why would he do that? The idea was dumb and John knew it.

"You haven't seen a large yellowish envelope with the newspaper address on it, have you Hans?" he asked.

Hans shook his head no.

"I have to get back outside," Jake said. "Just come on out when you're done, Hans."

John was surprised the Millers would leave Hans alone in the office, even if he was writing in Bibles. He was a German prisoner, after all. He wondered if Pete knew about this.

"John, I'm going to find my dad, to ask him if he knows anything about the envelope," Sarah said. "You coming?"

"I need to make a telephone call," John said. "I need to call the newspaper."

"Why?" Sarah asked.

"If the drawings were mailed, I want to tell them I'm not entering them, that there was a mistake."

Sarah put her hands on her hips. "You're at least going to enter the one of me, aren't you? You said your father was fine with that."

"If I enter the one of you, and I win, your face will be plastered across the newspaper. Have you thought of that?"

"Well, not really. But you said it's the only drawing you can enter."

John studied Sarah's face. "I don't know if you would like that kind of attention. All those people staring at your picture. Recognizing you when you go to town."

"You'll soon have me changing my mind," Sarah said. "Maybe I should be glad the envelope is lost."

"Try to find it anyway," John said. "And my mother's in the kitchen talking with your mom. Could you tell her she can go on to work? Tell her I'll give her the drawing later."

Sarah left and John began to poke around the office, hoping the envelope would jump out at him.

A tapping sound got his attention.

John turned around. Hans was so quiet John had almost forgotten he was there. John watched him tap the pen nib on the jar of ink, letting the excess ink drip back into the bottle.

"How many drawings are you missing?" Hans asked.

"Four. I know they're not the most important things in the world, but I hate not knowing where they are."

"It's not a good feeling to lose your work," Hans said. "I hope you find them."

The stiff change in Hans' voice made John pause. "Where are all your paintings? At your home?" John asked.

Hans finished writing a letter, ending it with a slight flourish. "They were at my home. And at school. But I am from Berlin. Our house was destroyed from one of the bombs that struck my city. I don't know if the school is still standing."

John hesitated, then asked, "Was your family hurt?"

"No, they were with relatives."

"Did you have a lot of paintings?"

Hans stopped writing. He looked up. "I had many paintings, yes. And drawings."

John shook his head. "Boy, I can't imagine how that would feel."

Hans gave a slight nod.

"But at least no one took your skill away, right?" John said, desperate to think of something positive. "You still have that. Do you draw much now? I guess it would be hard to paint in a prison camp, but . . ."

"It would be allowed. But I have no more desire to draw or paint. The first time I picked up a pencil to draw anything since I joined the army was when I did a little shading in your sketchbook."

"Why? I mean, how can you just stop like that?"

Hans let out a rough laugh. "Easy," he said. "The images in my mind these last few years are not ones I want to put on paper."

"Maybe it would help you to draw again. Maybe . . ."

"It feels good to do this pen and ink writing for now," Hans interrupted.

The hard look in Hans's eyes told John he'd said enough. John tried to imagine what it would be like to lose all of his drawings. Or what it would be like to live at a prison camp. Who would want to sketch with Nazi types like Dieter Klein watching you? Maybe it had been cruel to bring up drawing and painting to Hans. John wished he'd kept his mouth shut.

John shuffled through some more envelopes that were lying around the office before he gave up and sat down to watch Hans work.

"When are you heading home?" Hans asked.

"I get to stay until Wednesday."

"You sound happy about it," Hans said.

John shrugged his shoulders, slightly embarrassed that he seemed glad to be away from his family. "Well, if you have to work, this is an all right place to do it," he said.

Hans smiled. "That's true. It's the best work assignment I've had in the United States. Maybe anywhere."

"Where else have you been?" John asked.

"I fixed camouflage nets in Colorado and picked potatoes in Missouri. I was also at a prison camp in Virginia."

"What was it like? Was it hard?"

"It was hard sometimes. I appreciated getting out to work."

"How were you treated as a prisoner at the camps and all?"

Hans pushed his chair away from the desk. "I'm finished with these. I'm going back to the greenhouses. You coming or staying here?"

"I'll go with you," said John.

John thought maybe he'd asked too many questions again as they walked outside. He glanced up at the sky. It was much darker than when he'd arrived.

Hans bent down to pet Max, who had rushed up to greet them. Max rolled over on his back, his legs pointed up in the air, waiting for his muddy belly to be rubbed.

"You want to know what it's like to be a prisoner?" Hans asked after a moment. "I am grateful to receive food and shelter and I have never been tortured, so I cannot complain. During the war, the thought among my comrades was, if you're going to be captured, let it be by the Americans."

"Who would it be bad to be captured by?"

"There are many stories," Hans said. "It's difficult to know what is a lie or truth. But the Russian PWs were not always treated well by us and I did not want to be caught by a Russian." Hans shrugged. "The Japanese also have a reputation for being . . . very harsh. But I have no experience of being caught by either of them. There are cruel Americans, as well. But we heard our chances would be better with them, of being treated like a human being, especially if you were sent to the United States. This has been true for me."

"Oh," said John. "So you were actually glad to see American uniforms when you were captured?"

"I think I hear excitement in your voice, like this sounds like a great adventure. It was no great adventure to me."

Hans looked at John and gave a small smile. "I was not glad for anything at that moment, except that I was standing and breathing. I had just watched many friends die. They fell around me, on all sides. Some of their faces blown to bits. Some of them screaming from pain. There was no good cover. We fought until there were only three of us left and I knew it was over. I threw my rifle down and raised my hands, not knowing what would happen.

"And let me tell you, John," Hans said as he made a fist and covered it with his other hand, bringing it close to John's nose. "The fear that wraps around you at a time like that is like a physical pain—squeezing, squeezing your heart."

Hans took a step back and took off his cap. He tilted his face up to catch the large drops of water beginning to come down. "I love rain," he said.

"Yeah, it feels good." John wondered exactly how much Hans wanted to enjoy the rain, because he knew they were soon going to get drenched if they didn't move along.

"That fear," said Hans. "It didn't stop when I saw American uniforms. Every man has to make a decision in that moment. They could have killed me."

"What did happen?" asked John, as a crack of thunder echoed behind him.

"A sergeant stepped forward. He was a black man. Very tall. He offered me a cigarette. I will never forget him."

The rain began to come down harder. Hans stood still for several moments longer, his eyes closed as small streams ran down his face.

"Another soldier even gave me a chocolate bar." He laughed quietly. "I couldn't believe it. That was when I relaxed a little bit."

John smiled as they began to walk again. He felt water seep through the hole in his shoe.

"Did you take the cigarette?" he asked.

"Oh yes," said Hans. "The sergeant was offering me a gift. I stood in that spot and smoked it."

CHAPTER TWENTY-EIGHT

"John!" his father yelled from the porch. "You have a telephone call!"

John was hanging up laundry outside. He'd been home for more than a week now and felt like he was some kind of maid. He didn't complain, but he didn't like it. He cared for his dad during his mother's shift at the factory, did laundry, worked in the garden, cooked, and cleaned. His leg still hurt a lot, but that wasn't something he'd ever say out loud.

His dad spent most of his time in his room or out on the porch, reading. John still couldn't get used to seeing his dad reading a book in the middle of the day. Books on war and history. Or he'd look at issues of *Life* magazine, even though he'd yelled about not wanting to see the magazine lying around. A letter had come from Al, the combat artist his dad had served with. He was alive and nearby, in Delaware. One of his paintings was in the latest edition of the magazine. It was of a ship on fire. Men on fire. Men screaming and jumping into the water. John's dad stared at it for long periods of time. Did he recognize the faces? Sometimes John felt like tossing one of his comic books onto his dad's lap to break the silence, lighten things up a bit.

But today he wasn't up to taking on his dad's moods. On top of hanging up laundry, he was in the middle of making vegetable soup using the few vegetables that were in the garden—zucchini, tomatoes, and peppers.

"The key to soup is broth," Sarah had said when they'd spoken earlier. "Use a good soup bone with some meat on it." Too bad he didn't have a soup bone.

"Coming, Pop!" he yelled. He wondered if it was Sarah again, calling to check up on his cooking experiment in her amused but full-of-wisdom voice.

"John Witmer?"

"Yeah?"

"This is Robert Watson. I'm one of the judges for the newspaper art contest. We've decided on our top three finalists, and you're one of them.

Your drawing of the POWs and other farm workers picking tomatoes side by side is being considered for first place. Congratulations, son. You have a lot of talent."

"Thank you, sir." John smiled. He was talking to Robert Watson. The artist whose work he thought was amazing.

"Only the first place winner will get private art lessons, but the second and third place winners will receive art supplies, so no matter how this turns out you've already won something. The prize includes a beautiful set of oil paints. Have you worked much with oils?"

John's dad had gone back into his bedroom, but the door was open.

"No, I haven't really had the chance. But sir . . ."

"Yes?"

How could he do it? How could he turn this down? He'd go one more round with his dad. He wasn't too proud to beg.

"Nothing. Sorry. I don't know what to say."

"Well then, I have one more bit of news to pass on. We received so much wonderful artwork we've decided to exhibit all the pieces at the downtown library. We're going to announce the winners there at a little ceremony on opening night. I personally felt your drawing of the fire and the man lying on the ground was your best work, but it didn't tie as directly to the theme as we thought necessary. It can be on display at the exhibit, however. And the one of the girl in the victory garden was excellent as well, but we received so many drawings of victory gardens, we decided on something that stood out in a different way. In the drawing we chose of yours, each facial expression seemed to tell its own story. It showed an interesting dynamic of the war— POWs working alongside Americans on farms."

John was feeling more and more like a fraud. His dad would never let him do this. He wished they had chosen the one of Sarah. It would be so simple then.

"By the way, if you have any frames you can use for your drawings for the exhibit, that would be helpful, and they would protect your work."

"I'll have to see."

"All right then, John. We'll talk again soon."

"Thank you, sir. I'm honored that you chose me as a finalist."

John hung up the phone. He picked up an onion and began chopping. Chop. Chop. Chop. What a difference a little practice made. His culinary skills were humming along.

"Looking to lose a finger?" John hadn't heard his dad move up behind him.

"Nope."

"Who was on the phone?"

"A judge from the newspaper."

"You win?"

"I'm a finalist. With the wrong drawing, though. Ouch!"

"Put down that knife, boy. Look at you, you're bleeding all over the place. Put your finger under water."

His father rummaged through a drawer and cut up a long strip of cloth.

"Here. Wrap this around it."

John tried to wrap the cloth around his still bleeding finger, but his dad pushed his hand away.

"Let me do it. One thing that war taught me is how to wrap a bandage."

John noticed his dad's hands weren't shaking as he wound the cloth tightly around John's finger. That was a good sign at least.

"What'd you mean, the wrong drawing?"

John got a rag and started wiping the blood off the counter. He knew he was going to sound like a liar.

"Somehow several of my drawings got mailed to the newspaper. Sarah had them in an envelope in the office at their house. I guess it got mailed by accident. I called the newspaper and said I only wanted to enter the one you told me to, but my message didn't reach the right person, I guess. I swear, Pop. I told them I was only entering the one of Sarah in the garden."

"What's the picture of—that they like?"

"It's one of everyone picking tomatoes. In a greenhouse. Some PWs, Sarah, Dorothy and Kenny, Reuben."

"These names don't mean a thing to me."

"They're Miller kids, and Reuben is . . ."

"It doesn't matter. Is that PW in it that I saw at the farm? The one that's in all your other pictures?"

"He's not in all my other drawings. But yeah, he's in it."

His dad ran his hands down his thighs.

"I can't do it, boy. I can't stand it. Can't stand the thought of you working next to them, of you drawing them, making friends with them. Maybe that soldier is better than some. But it's too soon." His dad was shaking his head, back and forth.

"I understand, Pop, but you sit around here reading history books. Books on war. I'm just doing what those authors did! I'm just recording history. Marking it down as it happens. Just with drawings, not words. I'm not saying it's good or bad—I'm not making judgments!"

"You like these men. It comes out in your work. Don't deny it."

His dad pushed away from John and grabbed a book from the table. "I've said how I feel," he called out before going outside.

John stared at his watery, unappetizing soup simmering on the stove. At the very least he'd won oil paints! And his dad wouldn't let him accept them. If he withdrew, he'd never even know if he'd won first place. He'd never know if he could have had lessons with a famous artist.

"There's a purpose for everything," Sarah had told him during one of her preaching moods.

John wondered what great purpose she'd come up with for this situation. What purpose would be served from letting go of the greatest opportunity of his life?

CHAPTER TWENTY-NINE

John was up early the next morning, and climbed on his bike when he saw his mom's car turning into the driveway. She'd worked the night shift and had told him he could leave for the day after she got home. John was heading to the Millers. Days were long at home with his dad's spiritless, yet hard-nosed presence. He wanted to hear the hum of the farm—be part of the liveliness. He swerved around a squirrel that seemed to run straight for his tire. His wheels skidded on the gravel driveway, but he recovered in time to give his mom a wide berth as she handled the Chevy. She tooted the horn as they passed each other.

John hadn't told her he was a finalist in the contest. It would have been nice to watch her face light up at the news, but she'd go on about it and his dad wouldn't want to hear it. John knew he had to call the newspaper to withdraw, but every time he picked up the phone, he couldn't follow through. He kept wondering what would happen if he left his drawing in the competition. If he won, would Pop ever forgive him?

The Miller farm was oddly quiet when John arrived. No one was picking tomatoes. The cannery was still.

John knocked on the front door of the house. No answer. He walked around toward the barn. Sarah was poking at a fire in the pit. Dorothy and Kenny were gathering sticks.

"John!" Dorothy yelled when she saw him, dropping her armload of sticks and running toward him. She threw her arms around his waist, jumping up and down at the same time.

"We're getting ready for a chicken barbecue," she said. "And homemade ice cream! Can you stay?"

John looked up at Sarah.

"You're invited," she said. "We're having an early supper, so the PWs can join us." Sarah grinned. "Too bad you weren't around to help me catch the chickens."

"Yeah. Too bad."

"I helped her," said Kenny. "I'm faster'n Sarah at grabbing 'em. Right, Sarah?"

"You're fast, anyway," Sarah said.

"Where is everybody?" John asked.

"Working on my Uncle Harvey's farm, picking peaches. They needed an extra truckload of PWs and ended up with some of those scary ones," said Kenny. "They had to send an extra guard along."

"Mother won't say it, but I think she feels our regular PWs deserve a good meal after working around them all day," Sarah added.

"So everybody's coming back here to eat?" John asked. "Even the Nazi ones?"

"No, just our regular bunch. Pete says he'll manage it."

When the time came to barbecue the chicken, John offered to help, even if it was the last thing he felt like doing. Listening to Kenny talk about catching them, and looking at them on the grill, actually made his stomach turn.

Sarah picked up some tongs and started turning the chicken legs. The skin was beginning to turn crisp and brown.

"So, have you heard anything from the paper?" Sarah asked.

"The drawing of you wasn't selected for the final competition."

"And your father hasn't changed his mind about the other drawings?"

"No."

Sarah slapped the piece of chicken she was holding onto the wire mesh, making the other pieces of chicken jump. "I'm sorry you didn't win," she said, "but you're probably just as good as the artist offering the lessons, anyway." Sarah paused. "You're not telling me something," she said, studying his face.

"What kind of sauce is on this chicken?" he asked. "It smells great."

"My grandmother's recipe. I'll give it to you."

John listened to the sizzle of the juice from the chicken hitting the fire. He watched Sarah quickly turn each piece.

"I'm going to get some platters," Sarah said after a time. "It looks done."

John heard the rattle of the Miller truck coming up the lane. Jake pulled up by the barn, and the men immediately swarmed toward the smell of the barbecued chicken.

Fritz stood by the grill and took deep breaths, lifting his face toward the sky each time he inhaled. He began rubbing his shirt while mumbling in German.

Hans laughed.

"What's he doing?" John asked.

"He wants the smell in his clothing," Hans answered. "He says he can't remember when he's smelled anything so good."

When they sat down to eat, John settled into his usual spot between Hans and Dorothy and across from Sarah and Fritz. Wilhelm, the PW he didn't know very well, also joined them. The men looked tired and dirty but happy. John felt lucky he had come today. Looking at the golden crisp chicken, the deep red tomatoes, yellow corn on the cob, and pink sliced peaches helped ease his spirits a bit. And he admitted to himself what his father had pointed out. He liked being around these people.

Fritz was still talking.

"He says it's beautiful, like a painting," Hans said, as he too stared at the food.

Sarah jumped up. "I'm going to ask Jake to take a picture."

John was biting into his chicken, juice dribbling down his chin, when Jake snapped the first picture. Oh well, John thought. It would capture the moment he was eating the most delicious chicken he'd ever had while making a pig of himself. What the picture wouldn't capture was his struggle to keep the image of live chickens out of his head.

"Have you heard any news?" Hans asked John. "About the contest?"

John slowly swallowed his last bite of chicken. He thought about how he'd been evasive with Sarah, but with Hans he'd tell the truth. He wasn't sure why that was. Maybe because he knew Sarah would make a fuss. Maybe because he never knew when he'd see Hans again. There was only time for the absolute truth.

"I'm a finalist—one of the top three," John said. "The drawing of you all picking tomatoes in the greenhouse is the one they like. They told me I've at least won art supplies. But I can't accept them, and I can't win. My dad would hate the drawing."

"Why?"

John blushed. "He doesn't like anything I do if it has PWs in it."

"I read there's going to be an exhibit at the library."

"What about it?" John asked.

"You could still show some of your work, couldn't you?"

"I could only show the one of Sarah, and I don't see the point of it."

"Take advantage of the opportunity, John. One drawing is better than no drawings. You never know who will see it, or what it can do for you."

John bit into his corn so he wouldn't have to answer. He didn't want to go to the exhibit. They were going to announce the winners and it would be too hard to hear the names called out, and watch others receive the prizes, while he got nothing. Sarah could show the drawing of herself to people if she wanted. He'd give it to her.

When Reuben asked for a volunteer to turn the wooden handle on the ice cream maker, John got up to help. Hans followed him, taking over the second churn they had started.

"I want to tell you a true story," Hans said, as he began to crank the ice cream. "When I was sixteen, my father let me show several paintings in his gallery. It was my first time being part of an exhibit there and I wanted to show my best work. In the end, I was only satisfied with two paintings. But my father chose two additional paintings of mine to be part of the exhibit. I was very upset with him for displaying work that I felt was not good. The evening of the opening, a woman comes in, looks at one of the paintings I had not wanted to include, and immediately buys it. It was the only one I sold. I always wondered if she collected art for the Nazis. Hitler loves art, you know. And he prizes work like mine done in a classical style. She mentioned that Hitler would like my painting. But that's not the point of my story. You should show your work, John. Every drawing of yours is good. You have nothing to lose. Only something to gain."

John's mind was spinning. He understood what Hans was saying about the exhibit, even though he still didn't want to attend. But he was caught up in Hans's offhand remark about Hitler.

"What do you mean, your work may have been bought for the Nazis? That Hitler loves art?"

"He does. He collects art. And he is an artist himself, though he was turned down by an art school when he was young. He favors work that shows beauty, nature, family—the way he thinks they should look." Hans lowered his voice. "But he destroys art he doesn't like, such as modern art. And he steals art from the Jews. My father had a Jewish friend who had a large collection of paintings. Famous works. The Nazis took them. Stealing to capture beauty—those things don't seem to go together, do they?"

John kept turning the crank. Hitler was an artist? He hadn't known that. The thought made him sick. How could someone so evil be an artist?

John had thought about drawing the scene before him. But now he dismissed the idea. For the first time since he could remember he didn't feel like sketching. It would only be one more drawing he would have to keep hidden away. He was almost relieved. Maybe he would make his dad happy and put drawing aside. Maybe it wouldn't be so painful after all.

CHAPTER THIRTY

"What are you doing?" John asked.

"Measuring a piece of wood," his dad answered.

"I thought you weren't supposed to work out here by yourself." John didn't mean to sound harsh, but the doctor had said it wasn't safe for his dad to work alone because of the tremors in his arm.

His dad picked up a pencil and wrote down a measurement.

"I feel good today," he said. "And your mom said you need a frame."

"A frame? What are you talking about?"

"For the exhibit. That picture of Sarah was the same size as the drawing paper in your room, right?"

John nodded. He wondered if his dad had noticed that the blank drawing paper on his dresser was covered with dust. He hadn't worked on anything in a while.

"I don't need a frame, Pop. I'm not going to put it in the exhibit."

"Your mother's counting on it."

"I already know it won't win."

"She'll be disappointed, but it won't ruin her enjoyment of having you be a part of it. She wants to show off your work to her friends. You hear her talking about it."

John closed his eyes. He was still officially a finalist. In his mind he imagined going to receive his prize, hearing his name called out. The drawing of the PWs picking tomatoes would be hanging with a ribbon on it. He wondered if his dad would cause a scene if that happened. If he would take down the drawing. Rip it up.

Actually, his dad probably wouldn't go to the exhibit. He didn't go anywhere yet. John could win. His mother would witness it and be so proud, and his dad wouldn't be there to ruin it for her.

"How would you like an inlay on the top and bottom of the frame?

Something different—like this." His dad sketched a simple but elegant design on paper. "If we use a darker shade of wood, I think it would look good. It would stand out. I even have some matting we could use." He looked up at John. "I thought maybe the judges would change their minds, seeing your drawing of Sarah in a nice frame and all. Maybe they'd give that one first place instead."

John knew that wouldn't happen, but he nodded. "The inlay's nice, Pop. What board do you want? I'll cut it. It's been a while since I've done this. I need the practice."

John had seen his dad's hand shake when he put down the pencil. He couldn't leave him alone. And John didn't have the heart to argue about the frame or the exhibit. He hadn't thought his dad would help him succeed with art in any way, ever, in his lifetime. John thought he should savor the moment as best he could. He knew he only had a short time left to withdraw from the contest. But tomorrow was another day. He'd decide then what to do.

CHAPTER THIRTY-ONE

"Isn't that something? What a beautiful girl."

"Is that your son there, Eleanor? And the girl standing next to him looks like the girl in the drawing."

"Yes, it is. That's Sarah Miller." John could hear the excitement in his mother's voice. Watching her face made him glad he had gone along with being in the exhibit. And he had to admit the frame he and his dad had made helped his drawing stand out. With its oak grain pattern, and darker curved inlays, the frame itself was a piece of art.

"They act like we can't hear them," Sarah said.

"No, they're just having too much fun to care if we do," John answered. "And you enjoy listening to them. I just hope it doesn't make you too vain."

"Don't be ridiculous. They're not talking about me personally. They're talking about the way you drew me."

John shook his head. "How are they separate? You tell me I'm a good artist. That means the person I draw should be recognizable if that's what I'm going for. I didn't create a new person when I drew you."

Sarah smiled a wide smile. "Are you saying I'm beautiful?"

John reached up to rub the back of his neck, hoping it wouldn't turn red.

A man stopped in front of John's drawing. John used that as an excuse not to answer Sarah's question. John discovered he liked watching people look at his drawing. He found it fascinating to watch their expressions, to see their eyes move over it. But he also imagined it was rude, so he looked away and watched Sarah walk toward his mom.

"Excuse me," the man said. "Are you John Witmer?"

"Yes, sir," John answered, turning around.

The man turned back to the drawing. "You capture the confidence of the young lady. She looks proud of her garden, proud of the land she is standing on, even a little proud of herself."

John grinned. "That's Sarah."

"I'm also admiring this frame. Who made this for you?" The man gently ran a finger over one of the inlays.

"My father and I made it, in his woodworking shop."

"Would you be willing to make more? I buy a fair number of frames. I would be quite interested in purchasing some of these. I'd want each one to be a little different. It looks like you could do that."

"We could," said a deep voice behind them.

John swung around and saw his father.

"Pop," was all he could say. He stared at his dad sitting in his wheelchair, a thin blanket covering his lap. "How did you get here? When did you get here?"

"Just now. I got a surprise visit from this fellow here, standing behind me. He about gave me a heart attack when he showed up. John, meet Al Fraser, the craziest combat artist there is."

Al stuck out his hand. "It's an honor," he said.

John shook his hand and then glanced over at the man he'd been talking to. "Excuse us, sir. This is my father, Ted Witmer, and his friend, Al Fraser."

John couldn't believe he was introducing his dad, or Al Fraser. The man holding onto the handles of his dad's wheelchair looked too young to be so accomplished, with his brown hair and bangs, and a scattering of pimples on his face.

"Robert Watson," the man said, reaching out to shake hands with both Al and John's dad. "You have a talented son."

"Well, I don't know anything about drawing, but this one looks pretty good to me," his dad said.

"It's getting a lot of attention," said Mr. Watson.

Robert Watson. John stared at the tall, balding man. He guessed he was in his fifties. John hadn't recognized his voice. He sounded different than he had on the phone when he'd told John that he was a finalist in the contest. Standing next to two great artists, John found himself tongue-tied. He couldn't think of a thing to say.

"You're Robert Watson? Painter and sculptor?" Al asked animatedly.

"I am. And I must say, I admire your work, Mr. Fraser. I saw some paintings of yours at the Metropolitan Museum of Art last year. That was the best war art exhibit I've ever seen. I spent hours there."

Mr. Watson glanced at the podium. "Well, I need to keep moving," he said. "If you write down your business address and phone number, I'll be in touch about ordering some frames, if you're interested in that kind of business."

John's dad nodded.

"And John," he said, smiling. "If you'd like to stop by my studio sometime,

I'd be happy to show you around. I have a couple of drawings you might like to see, as they are similar in style to your own work. And while we're at it, I could show you the paintings I'm intending to frame. Maybe looking at them would help inspire the frame designs."

"Sure," John said. "That'd be great." John watched him walk away. He had an invitation to Robert Watson's studio. Incredible.

John could hear his mother's laughter as she made her way toward him, her two friends by her side. Faye and Wilma both had sons who were fighting in the war, and they began to interrogate his dad about what it was really like. Amazingly, he didn't seem to mind talking to them.

John wandered around the room, examining the other entries. There were a lot of drawings of victory gardens. John could see why the judges wanted something more unique.

"Your dad told me about this contest, so I thought I'd visit and see more of your work at the same time," Al said, as he fell into step beside John. "He showed me that one you drew of your mom."

"I had other drawings for this contest that were better," John said, "but I didn't get to enter them."

"I know," Al said. "I gave your dad a hard time about that, too. I told him that keeping you from doing something you're naturally good at doesn't make much sense. I don't get the problem. I said maybe he wanted to be an artist himself and somebody discouraged him, so he's just feeling mean about it." Al barked out a short laugh. "He didn't like that, let me tell you."

John smiled. "I bet."

"But looking at the frame you both made tells me he does have an artistic eye, whether he likes it or not. I'm guessing his furniture has beautiful detail."

"Most of it is simple and sturdy. But when someone wants a fancy piece, he can do it." John looked into Al's amused eyes. "Pop's had a hard time. I can understand why he doesn't like PWs, why he doesn't want me drawing them."

"I told him if you met some decent German PWs, good for you. It'll improve your view of the world. And anything good that can come out of this war is worth hanging on to. Many of them are just regular folk, like we are. Your dad knows that. He's angry right now, and I can't say I blame 'im."

John wondered how his dad had responded to that. This man didn't seem the least bit afraid to say what he thought, yet his dad seemed happy to have him around.

"I'll tell you what, John. Meeting you sheds some light on how he treated me over there."

"What do you mean?"

"Your dad was always looking out for me—by yelling at me, mostly." Al laughed again. He had a strange laugh, John thought. Like a loud belly laugh that stops abruptly.

"We'd be attacked, and I'd think, time to draw. He'd holler at me to take cover, which I did—just not always fast enough for his liking. I had to get a few things down on paper first." Al grinned. "I really made him mad."

"What do I have to do with that?"

"We look a bit alike, don't you think? I got a few years on you, but I look young for my age, so they tell me. Me standing there with a sketchpad during combat? I think he was yelling at you as much as he was yelling at me."

"What was it like, trying to draw while fighting was going on?" John asked.

"Terrifying sometimes. But I just tried to concentrate on my job. After the chaos was over, I was always glad I'd hung in there. It was my chance to speak for those men."

"Time to announce our winning artists," said a woman's voice from the podium.

"Good luck, John," Al said. "I'll catch you later."

Sarah joined John as he found a place along a wall. "Want to move forward so we can see better?"

"No. But you can."

The third and second place winners were announced. Then, "And first place goes to Lena Earley for her drawing of the high school students and their tin drive!"

John clapped and watched a skinny girl who looked about his age step up on the podium. She was smiling shyly, but John could tell she was thrilled. Who wouldn't be?

Sarah squeezed his arm. "I'm sorry."

"It's okay, Sarah. Really." Mr. Watson shook Lena's hand. "Her drawing was good. I noticed it earlier. She deserves it."

Sarah opened her mouth to comment, when John's mother grabbed her and gave her a hug. "I'm so sorry you two didn't win," she said. She released Sarah and wrapped her arms around John. "I was so sure you would." John thought his mom must be building up muscles at the factory. He couldn't move from her tight grasp.

"Isn't that something?" Faye said. "I just don't know how it can be you didn't take first place, John."

"It's all right," John said. "But thanks. I'm glad you like my work."

John glanced at his dad. He was staring up at John's picture. John wondered if he was studying the drawing or the frame.

"I have to go, John," Sarah said, pulling him aside. "You were brave tonight."

"I wouldn't put it that way."

"Maybe you'll have other chances for lessons."

"Maybe I will."

Sarah blinked and looked away.

"Sarah," he said, touching her arm. "It's all right. The hardest thing was making the phone call to pull out my other drawing. But tonight was full of surprises. The judge invited me to visit his studio. He wants us to make frames for him. And my dad left the house for the first time. I think he enjoyed himself, too. And he brought a friend who's a famous combat artist. It's all unbelievable."

Sarah smiled. "That's good, John."

John met her eyes. He had drawn them proud and challenging, the way they usually appeared. He wished her eyes held that look now, instead of sadness.

"Can you work this week at all?" Sarah asked. "We could use you to pick tomatoes if your leg can take it."

"I could pick for a while—maybe in a couple of days, when my mom has off." John looked around at the crowd of people. "How many people do you think came here tonight?"

"I don't know, maybe a hundred. It was a lot."

John nodded. "I wish Hans could see the exhibit, but I'll tell him about it. He'll want to know what happened."

CHAPTER THIRTY-TWO

August 1944
Fort Indiantown Gap, Pennsylvania
Prisoner of War Camp

"You're a painter?" Fritz asked, his words heavy with surprise.

"Yes, I'm a painter." Hans looked sideways at Fritz.

"May I watch a bit?"

Hans shrugged. "I don't care," he said, as he worked the blue paint into the rough white paper. It seeped across the top, becoming sky on a languid summer day.

The feel of the smooth wooden paintbrush handle took him back to Germany, when he was a teenager with talent in a prestigious art program.

John would be pleased he was painting again. John had been thunderstruck that he had given up art. "How could you just stop like that?" he had asked.

Hans smiled slightly. As if there had been a choice when he was in combat. "I painted with a rifle," he had almost said.

Hans began painting neat rows of corn, leaves arching down on stalks climbing upward toward the heavens. Hans didn't know how he felt about heaven. He believed there was hell, though. At least hell on Earth. He'd had a taste of that.

Working on the farm had made him believe in basic human kindness again. The people there had allowed him to feel like a person with a little bit of goodness left in his soul.

Hans wanted to stay in touch with the Millers, Reuben, John. He likely wouldn't be allowed to write to them while he was a POW. But after the war ended, would they want to hear from him? He shook his head. How could he question that? They would welcome his letters.

Even John, who had once looked at him with pointed hatred, had become a friend. No person who studied people the way John did, who worked so hard at getting their emotions, their personalities just right on paper, would be able to hang on to hatred when sorrow and pain so blatantly looked back at him.

Hans had noticed that his own eyes had changed over the course of John's drawings. A bit of light, of curiosity--of normalcy-had appeared in the later drawings. He had lost that guarded look. It was a curious thing to see.

He wondered what the future held and how long it would take for him to return to being the man he had been only a few weeks ago. Maybe his experience at the farm would protect him.

The prison camp was usually quiet at this time in the evening. Hans was painting in the fading light. He would finish the painting by the dim light in the latrine if he had to. He didn't have much time, and he felt driven to get it done.

CHAPTER THIRTY-THREE

"Leave those chickens alone."

Sarah whirled around. "Are you trying to scare me to death?"

John laughed. "No. I was just telling you to leave the chickens alone."

"I'm letting them out, if you must know." Sarah turned around and unlatched the gate to the pen.

"Why?"

"So they can eat grass, take mud baths, get exercise. Happy chickens are healthier and lay better eggs. These birds actually have a good life."

"Until it's their time."

"Everybody has one. And since when do you care so much about the life of a chicken?"

"Since I had to look one in the eye, I guess."

For a moment John watched his mother drive out the farm lane on her way to the sewing factory. He glanced down as he walked through the grass toward the house. "Why is this one following me?"

Sarah looked over. One bird was walking quietly next to John, ignoring the other chickens, which had scurried past them. Sarah smiled. "She must like you."

They reached the house and Sarah hurried up the porch steps. "Be right back," she said.

John sat on the bottom step. The chicken wandered closer, stopping several feet in front of him.

"What do you want?" John asked out loud.

The chicken squawked, causing her red, wobbly chin to shake. But she kept her black eyes on John.

John took in the white tuft of hair on top of the bird's head. He looked at the pattern the white and brown feathers made, wrapping around her body.

"You're actually kind of pretty," John said. "Though I'm not sure I like you staring at me."

"Chickens can make good pets," Sarah said, joining John on the step. "They're loyal and intelligent."

With Sarah there, the bird seemed to lose interest in John. She walked regally over to some dirt and began to rub her feathers in it.

"Where are the PWs this morning?"

Sarah fidgeted with her dress, running a finger over the flowered pattern on her knee.

"Sarah?"

"The PWs . . . they're gone, John."

Sarah's tone made John uneasy.

"What do you mean? At your uncle's farm again?"

Now Sarah looked up, the warning in her eyes matched her fidgeting hands. "No. They were transferred to another camp. Maybe our government doesn't like them getting too comfortable. Or maybe they were needed for another work assignment. It will be the fourth camp Hans has been to."

John felt like he'd been hit hard in his gut. Like all the air had instantly been sucked from his body. John rose slowly to his feet and walked aimlessly around the yard. His overwhelming sense of loss took him by surprise.

He took a few steps in the direction of the cannery, able to make out the blackened part of the floor where the fire had occurred. He crouched down in the grass and pressed his fingers to his eyes.

What had kept a lid on his emotions—what kept life bearable—was coming to the Miller farm. Every time he worked with the PWs there were laughs, stories, and oddly, a feeling of belonging, even though he didn't understand half of what was said unless Hans translated for him. There was camaraderie between them all, and a profound gratefulness just for being here.

And John acknowledged to himself that Hans had been a good friend—a true friend. No one had ever understood him better, or taught him more. He wondered if he'd ever admit that out loud to anyone in his lifetime.

"When I was fourteen, my best friend was a PW," John whispered to the chicken that had come up to stand in front of him. John turned and walked back to Sarah.

"Did you know this was going to happen?"

"We learned of it a few days ago. Their last day here was yesterday."

"Where were they sent? Is it a good camp?"

"I don't know. Everyone was sad, though—the men, my parents. Me." Sarah nudged his shoulder. "Now you. But here," Sarah said. "Hans asked that I give you this."

Sarah handed him a rough-looking book. Its cover was made of thin cardboard. John opened it to a page with slanted, neat handwriting.

To John,
    An artist of rare talent, wise and brave, beyond his years.
    You will find your way.
    Your friend, Hans

Underneath was a drawing of John with his sketchbook. A quote followed.
    Whatever you can do, or dream you can, begin it!
    Boldness has genius, power, and magic in it.
    —Johann Wolfgang von Goethe

John swallowed. His fingers shook as he turned the page. A pencil sketch of Sarah and Dorothy, sitting at a picnic table, had a note on its opposite page. "Think of how to have texture in every drawing. I used the point and the side of my pencil. I used my eraser to smudge the shadows."

The next page was a charcoal sketch of the house. Then a watercolor of the cornfield and baskets of tomatoes, set off by a cool blue sky. "I'll always remember my first taste of sweet corn. I was sure you were joking with us."

John couldn't stop turning the pages. "When did he do this? Where did he get paints? I don't understand."

"He drew the one of Dorothy and me during lunch a couple of days ago. He didn't say what it was for, though. The others he must have done at the prison camp. He said they had some art supplies there."

John nodded. Pain and happiness and gratitude all welled up in him at the same time. Hans had started drawing and painting again. Why? For him?

One page had a message from Fritz in German. "Do you know what this means?" John asked.

Sarah moved closer to John and peered at the writing.

"It looks like a poem. It rhymes in German. It says something about tomatoes ripening, corn stalks waving in the fields. It seems to be capturing memories from his time here."

John stared at a drawing of himself and Sarah, Reuben and Jake, and four of the PWs, including Hans and Fritz.

"He drew that from a photograph. Remember when my dad took some pictures? He gave Hans one."

John nodded.

The last page looked like a letter.

Dear John,
    My life was changed this summer. The Millers, Reuben, and you gave me new hope and faith in human beings.
    You are a strong boy, John. I admired your strength. I know life was not easy for you.

And with a couple of old pencils and paper, you drew beautiful lines that told stories. You made me want to draw again. I don't know what will happen next, but I feel like I have an old friend with me when I draw in the evenings. For this I thank you.

The summer of 1944 I will remember as one of the best in my life. God bless you.

Hans

John smiled. He closed the book, running his fingers along its rough edges.

"We gave him our address," Sarah said. "He said he'd try to write to us after the war is over."

Sarah and John sat silently, shoulders barely touching. Sarah kicked off her shoes and made patterns with her toes in the dry dirt.

"In a few months Ben is enlisting in the army," John said.

"I'm sorry."

"He'll be ready to go. Part of him wishes he wouldn't have to, I guess, but we need to win this war."

"I just wish it would end. It's so awful," Sarah said. Sarah pushed at John's foot with the tip of her toe. "Take your shoes off, it feels good."

"Don't we have to start working?"

"We will. Can you draw with your feet?"

"Sarah, I swear, you ask the strangest questions sometimes."

"You shouldn't swear. Can you? Draw with your feet?"

"Sure," John said. "I'm brilliant at it." John kicked his dusty work shoes aside and drew a few quick lines with his big toe.

"There," he said. "Your turn."

Sarah drew a circle inside the tic-tac-toe board. "Very original."

They took turns making marks with their toes until Sarah filled in the last space. "No one ever wins this game."

John pushed her foot aside. "Watch me," he said.

"Hey!" Sarah laughed, and tried to stop him from erasing her mark.

"Ow!" John yelled, pulling his leg back.

"Oh John, I'm sorry. But that was your own fault." Sarah leaned down to look at John's calf. "It looks better," she said. "How does it feel? I mean in general, not right after it's been bumped."

John shrugged. "Sore. Ugly, isn't it?"

"It's not so bad." Sarah looked up. "School starts in a couple of days. You're coming back, aren't you? Will you be able to ride your bike that distance twice a day?"

"Yeah. I'd go crazy if I couldn't go back to school."

John looked through the book again, then handed it to Sarah. "Can you keep that in a safe place for me?"

"Sure. Just let me know when you want it again."

Sarah stood up. "I'll run it in. Should I tell my mother you'll be here for supper? You're welcome to stay." Sarah grinned. "Or maybe you won't want to eat with us. We're having chicken pot pie."

John glanced at the chicken that had followed him and was now eating grass close by. "As long as it's not my friend over there," he said. "I think I'll name her Molly."

"Who would have thought?" Sarah murmured as she walked up the porch steps. "John Witmer making friends with a chicken."

QUESTIONS FOR DISCUSSION

1. During WW2, combat artists lived with soldiers overseas and drew and painted war scenes. Do you feel it is important to see images of the realities of war? How do you think it would affect you to see paintings of war today—capturing exactly what is happening, including injuries and death?

2. How do paintings differ from photography in depicting scenes from war? Does one medium affect your emotions more than the other?

3. Do John's feelings about the war change?

4. Was John's father justified in keeping John from submitting all of his drawings to the newspaper contest? Why or why not?

5. The US closely followed the Geneva Convention during WW2, an international agreement that states how prisoners of war should be treated. The hope was that the Germans would treat American POWs in the same manner. Was this a good policy? How did it affect how the US prison camps were run?

6. What choice do you think you would make if you had to face death or fight for a cause you did not believe in?

Donna J. Stoltzfus grew up in New York City, but often visited Lancaster County, Pennsylvania, where she had extended family of both Mennonite and Amish heritage. Stoltzfus earned a bachelor's degree from Goshen College and a master's degree from New York University. She and her husband have raised their three children in Lancaster County.